To Robert Emmerson Tones who would have so loved the opportunity to do this himself.

Robin Tones

MURDER ON THE ANGKOR EXPRESS

AUSTIN MACAULEY PUBLISHERS™
LONDON • CAMBRIDGE • NEW YORK • SHARJAH

Copyright © Robin Tones 2022

The right of Robin Tones to be identified as author of this work has been asserted by the author in accordance with section 77 and 78 of the Copyright, Designs and Patents Act 1988.

All rights reserved. No part of this publication may be reproduced, stored in a retrieval system, or transmitted in any form or by any means, electronic, mechanical, photocopying, recording, or otherwise, without the prior permission of the publishers.

Any person who commits any unauthorised act in relation to this publication may be liable to criminal prosecution and civil claims for damages.

This is a work of fiction. Names, characters, businesses, places, events, locales, and incidents are either the products of the author's imagination or used in a fictitious manner. Any resemblance to actual persons, living or dead, or actual events is purely coincidental.

A CIP catalogue record for this title is available from the British Library.

ISBN 9781398444713 (Paperback)
ISBN 9781398444720 (ePub e-book)

www.austinmacauley.com

First Published 2022
Austin Macauley Publishers Ltd®
1 Canada Square
Canary Wharf
London
E14 5AA

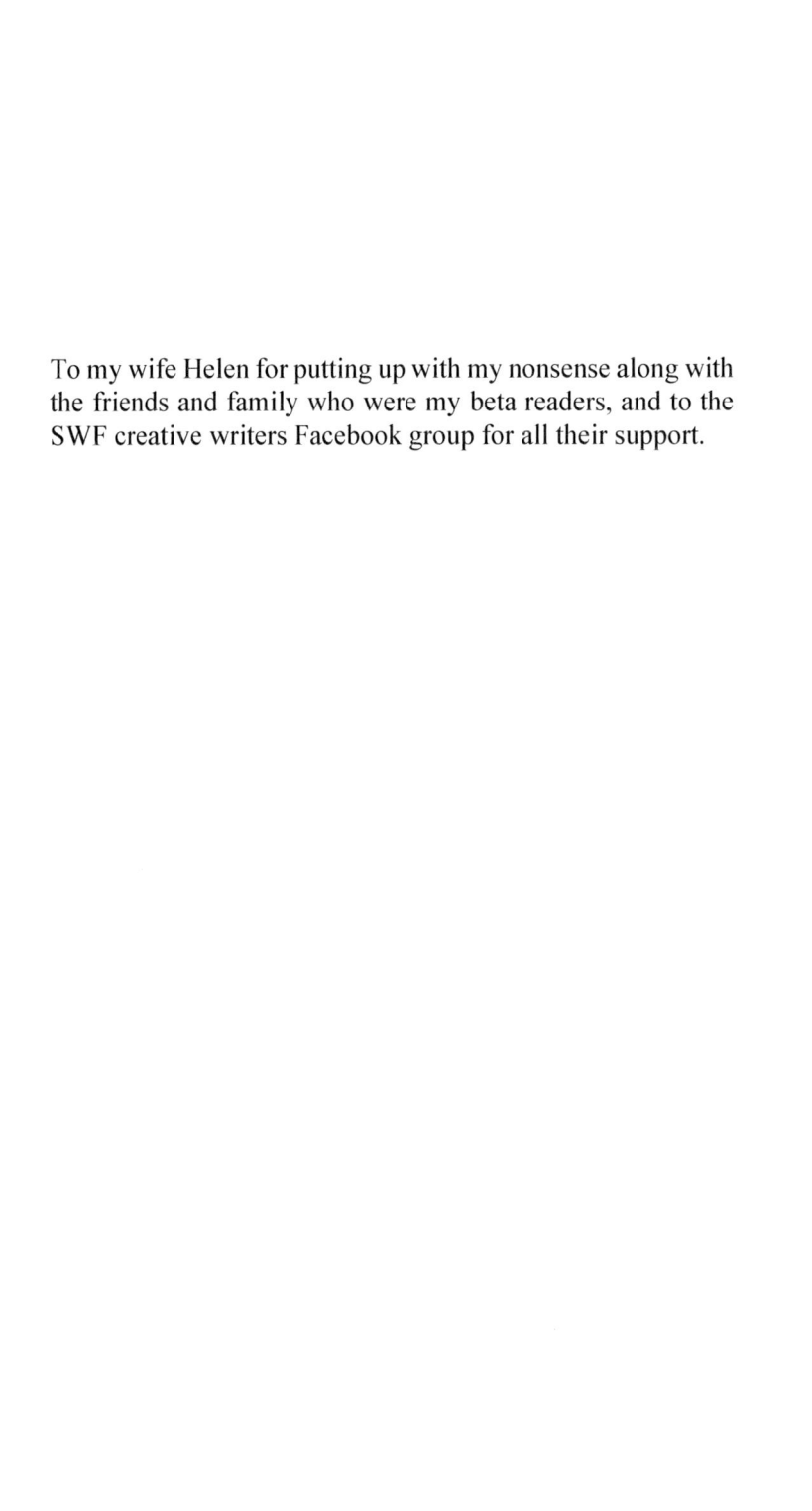

To my wife Helen for putting up with my nonsense along with the friends and family who were my beta readers, and to the SWF creative writers Facebook group for all their support.

A Stabbing

I took the call just before lunch, a stabbing on a tourist bus, one dead, possibly murder. Usually, the foreigners were handled by the security police. I pick up my mobile and message my colleague Samnang, no need getting all worked up and missing lunch just to hand the case over later. In the past, I would have called his secretary, but everyone is on their mobiles nowadays, so no point using the internal phones. To get things done, you need to know everyone's private number, that's how we expedite matters in Cambodia, "around corners".

Samnang texts me back immediately, he says he is too busy with the counter-revolution so I should handle this one. Criminal law is always the junior partner; no one cares about actual crime as there are so many far more interesting and lucrative jobs to be done. Picking up my gun and police hat I call over to Sergeant Munny to drive me to the Siem Reap Western Bus Terminal. I've never used my gun in anger in over twenty years in the police. My hat is my real tool; it demonstrates my power in our authoritarian Kingdom.

We take a moped, as I can do this without filling in any paperwork. It's also quicker navigating the chaotic traffic at this time of the day. Everyone will be going somewhere. Cambodia works on the anthill principle, just keep moving.

A simple stabbing does not normally require the personal attendance of a chief inspector, even if the victim is a foreigner. There is something in my stomach, however, that tells me this isn't going to be a run-of-the-mill case. On the upside, how hard can it be to find a killer on a bus? Hopefully, it is open and shut. I like the idea of a quick arrest and a boost to my personal conviction rate.

Munny efficiently manoeuvres us through the streets, missing potholes, food vendors and vacuous tourists confident that a mere Cambodian would not dare run them over. Our hospital bears testament to the fallacy of this supposition. We pull up at the unpaved, over-crammed yard which has been designated by the local tour companies as a bus terminal by the addition of a rusty blue sign. The official government Central Bus Terminal is closer to the centre but charges taxes. There are also clean working "Western" toilets here, the only thing tourists ever care about.

The dilapidated blue bus with "Angkor Express Limousine Coach" plastered along the side is parked on the edge of the yard. It is cordoned off by official police blue and white tape. I will compliment the local boys for this later; where they got the tape from, I have no idea. Sergeant Munny leaps off the bike to discover what is happening. I have more important duties to attend to, primarily to get an iced coffee with sweet milk, although this is hardly a substitute for lunch.

'Well, Sergeant?' I ask on his return.

'Sir, the body is still on the bus untouched, and the passengers are currently confined in the waiting room.'

It is a cool day today, a smidge over thirty-two degrees with only eighty percent humidity.

'How long have they been held?' I know how impatient, and intolerant of delay visitors can be.

'About an hour so far. They are asking for access to the toilets,' he replies. Munny lacks empathy. I can imagine the desperation that the tourists will be suffering. The lack of relief that they must need after the bone-jarring six-hour ride from Battambang, down our somewhat imperfect highways. I had intended to keep myself at arm's length, but it looks like I will need to be more personally involved. Decisive action is expected from leaders. Munny has rounded up the six local policemen who are managing the situation. When you only pay officers four dollars a day, you can afford plenty of feet on the street.

'Well done men, good job,' I address them in a shady spot outside the waiting room. 'Now escort the passengers to the toilets and get some air-con into that room. I am going to see the body. Can I just confirm that no one has touched it?' Their heads nod like feeding chickens as they mumble back. Generally, policemen don't get to speak to their leaders directly. I like to think I cut a dashing figure for them, as I am six foot, which is tall for a Cambodian, and I am impeccably dressed in my uniform with a gamut of shiny medals.

A young man jumps forward. 'Private Cheng, sir. Once we had checked that the man was dead, we left the body untouched. I managed to withdraw his wallet without moving anything else, here it is, sir!'

We don't have the best police academies in Cambodia as high-quality trainers are hard to come by. All good policemen are needed on the streets, not on campus. We do, however, have a country that is addicted to American TV shows which are constantly aired on SingMeng, our leading provider. You will often hear our guys using USA police codes to each other on their mobiles. Watching these shows has dramatically improved our own police protocols.

Sergeant Munny looks miffed that he has not been given the wallet. The young Cheng has made sure he got the glory, and by using plastic gloves he was certainly to be credited as I doubt Munny would have been so meticulous.

'Do we have a name?'

'His ID card says he is Leap Son. He is from the Krachie province, a rice trader. The card is in this evidence bag, Chief Inspector.' The bright young Cheng continues to impress.

'Not a tourist, then?' I ask them, expecting no answer.

Taking the wallet, I go to the bus. As the men trudge off to manage the passengers, I shout back, 'Oh and get them some bottles of water, Sergeant Munny has some cash.' Here I am giving Munny a small opportunity to make a margin, as the water costs will no doubt be more on the receipt than he pays to the trader. It is by little measures like these that the police force is covertly rewarded.

As I am just about to enter the bus, a well-heeled man accosts me. 'When do I get my coach back, I am late for the return trip already?' he fumes.

I look at him, he is intimating a move to his wallet, a universal signal that he will make my efforts "worth it". Luckily, as a chief inspector, I am not only better paid than Sergeant Munny, I also have far more lucrative backhand arrangements.

'I suggest you co-operate fully with my investigations or this bus could be in the station for a month! I am the Chief Inspector of the Criminal Police Force of Siem Reap.' The man steps back, stunned. 'Do you want my men to inspect your wretched bus for roadworthiness?' When dealing with local entrepreneurs, it is often best to make sure they know who is in charge.

'But, oh, sorry Chief Inspector,' with eyes down and palms up in submission. I have his full, cowed attention.

'Honestly, if this is murder, we can hardly let you put the bus right back on the road, so get a substitute in.' Giving some realistic advice after a reprimand often goes down well with reasonable men, and you never know when you may need their help in the future. I have a back pocket full of useful people.

Backing off and bowing slightly he adds submissively, 'anything I can do to help, Chief Inspector.' With honour satisfied he leaves to scrape up another rusting Chinese bus to call a Limousine Express. I climb the disgracefully dirty stairs, pulling myself up past the tattered blue plastic seats, to inspect the scene.

This is not a full-sized coach; it is called a "mini" in the trade, which normally means it goes faster than a big bus, with far fewer stops and is generally more comfortable. It's still a long way from the description given in the local adverts, and definitely not an express. For its type, this pile of junk has a conventional layout with five sets of two chairs either side of the corridor and a backbench of five seats.

The body is scrunched against the window, two rows back on the left-hand side.

Lifting a fold in the voluminous black coat, I see the handle of a dagger. Only the hilt is left exposed, I guess that the blade is about ten centimetres. Around the wound there is no obvious blood, nor is there any on the seat or floor beneath.

So, we have a laceration big enough to slaughter a calf and less blood than from a paper cut.

The victim has a conical bamboo hat on, draped over his face as if in an attempt to sleep. These coolie hats are popular with the tourists and surprisingly afford efficient shade from our tropical sun. I tip it so that I can match the ID card to the face. In reality, all I can tell is that the card and man were both old; whether they went together any further than this is a big question.

He has long hair, which I lift to get a look at his skin tone. Doing this, I can see the broken ends of a leather thong which is around his neck. Could he have been strangled, then stabbed? This is becoming uncomfortably complex. I had hoped for an easy, obvious death of a drunken peasant, preferably with blood all over their hands. I have here a dead man with multiple assaults and no doubt a lot of paperwork. If there had only been foreigners on the bus, I could try again to pass it over to my colleagues. This now looks as if it is going to be a long day.

General Cho

'Munny, get off your phone and get our CSI team down here! We need to transfer the body to the morgue. This one requires a real autopsy, as it isn't a stabbing, but something far more sinister.'

Whoever was in the seats behind the man is my prime suspect for a garrotting. I have to work out where each of the passengers was sitting. Briefly, I consider that there may be a larger conspiracy – possibly that they all did it. A plot lifted from my hero Agatha Christie; possibly a Poirot story? Alas, no, this is most likely a simple murder committed for some petty personal reason. Murder is often so pointless. I don't think I need to worry about splitting all the tourists up to stop them from supporting each other's stories. If I interview them as a group, it will ensure that no-one can lie, and hopefully will save a huge amount of time.

The waiting room is now well air-conditioned, to my relief. The fourteen suspects are seated around the room drinking bottled water. It looks like Sergeant Munny has spent our entire refreshments budget, as there are also tins of expensive American sodas and even a beer for the driver. On the wall is a large sheet of A1 which looks like it has been ripped from a flip chart pad. You don't see those outside the general staff conference rooms.

Someone has drawn a diagram of the bus with the various seats and the door marked. A cross marks the spot of our victim, Leap Son.

'I set out a plan so you could mark who sat where, Chief Inspector.' The young Cheng says; he is quite a find. As I go to say well done, he presents me with a black marker pen.

'How is your English, Cheng?' So far, we have been talking solely in Cambodian and although foreigners sometimes can speak Cambodian, it is rare. I want to keep my English fluency quiet until I need to speak directly; you never know what I might overhear.

'I received a distinction at school, sir. Shall I ask them where they sat and if they moved?'

'Yes, go ahead Cheng, mark them up on the board.'

Cheng circles the room asking who had sat in which seats and where they were from. I match each of the passenger groups up with the pile of passports the men have collected. The two middle-aged French ladies sitting together swathed in floral patterns look most upset whilst the young blond American casually flexes himself against the wall. An older English couple complain that they had booked the front seats and that the young American had taken their places. In the end, they had sat in the penultimate seats to the rear, either side of the gangway. They explained that the chairs themselves were so uncomfortable they needed two each. From the size of them, I think they needed more. I don't understand how these Westerners get so fat.

The driver explains that a young couple of Cambodians got off the bus on the outskirts of town. He looks into the ground and rubs his yellow-stained fingers, seemingly desperate for an injection of nicotine. He swore that he didn't know who they were, that they had just told him very specifically where to be dropped off. I can tell by his body language that he is lying, evasive and scared, whether that is because of my hat or a more nefarious reason I can't judge. Did he have the opportunity to kill Mr Son? I will make sure we ask the passengers when he ventured back onto the bus.

Trying the well-used inquisitorial tactic of the force, I ask, 'Did you kill your passenger?'

He looks up at me, clearly shocked by the enquiry, 'No, no, no.'

'Then why are you so scared? You are sweating like a fat American in a sauna.'

'I'm sorry, sir, I'm sorry, but my papers have not been renewed. I am using my brother's.'

As ever it is the most likely reason that causes problems. Our licensing department is far behind on paperwork, even mine has been out of date for six months awaiting recertification. 'Go and tell the Sergeant, I'm sure he can work things out.' There's a flashing smile from the man and a visible exhalation of breath. He obviously knows that Munny will let him off with a judicious fine, which will no doubt include a "tip".

I move back to considering the rest of the suspects: A newlywed Vietnamese couple; two Dutch youngsters travelling together; a middle-aged married French couple and a pair of Romanians, of all things. Reporting back, the men tell me that they all say the same thing, which is that they had neither sat next to nor talked to the victim and definitely no one had seen the murder. Leap Son was on the bus as they arrived and was only found to be dead by the driver as they got off. He had then raised the alarm, so couldn't have been the killer. It feels good to start ticking the suspects off.

No murderer is jumping out and saying, "It's me", which alas, rarely happens. More importantly, no one is pointing their finger at another passenger. I assumed the English would blame the French no matter what they had seen, but I have to admit my mass interview approach is failing. There is no easy answer. Reluctantly, I will have to start individual statements. Surely the cord could only have been administered to Leap Son by the passengers immediately behind him. So it must be the French ladies?

'Cheng, I have my sergeant sorting out the crime scene, so I will need you to help me with the interviews. Don't worry, I will settle with your boss later. Are you up for it?'

'Yes, sir!' says the enthusiastic young pup.

'Shit!' I exclaim, as a text appears on my phone from my boss, Cyril Meng, the Chief of Police. "Come back now." Cyril is a man of few words, so such a message is not to be taken as an insult. Both he and I, as the only Catholics in the Siem Reap force, have a special bond.

Leaving Cheng to organise the first statements, I drive the moped myself. Dumping it at the station in the hands of a young private. Leaving him to find a parking space which is like playing reverse Jenga. I stride into Cyril's office.

'What is so important to bring me off this...' standing in the corner is a short, fat man in green army fatigues with a very impressive hat.

'Sorry I didn't see you there, General,' I stutter. Although not part of our chain of command, the general is significantly senior to Cyril. Technically, Cambodia is a parliamentary constitutional monarchy, and therefore the army is simply another state agency, don't you believe it. If the army asks you to jump, you answer, "How high?"

'I understand that a local has been stabbed on a tourist bus, Chief Inspector Suon?' With his finger pointing and chin thrust out, this is more of a verbal lunge than merely a question.

'Yes, General.' Information travels very quickly, it seems. 'I asked Chief Inspector Samnang if he was taking the case, but he told me that it was a criminal affair.'

'Quite right, not all tourists are subversives; some can simply be criminals. We don't want this affair to be in the news now, do we?' He looks deeply into my eyes, beaming. I really wish he wouldn't smile at me; a shudder ripples down my spine.

My mouth becomes dry. 'I'm sure that news coverage is not my department, General. It's hard to think it won't be covered by the press if a tourist is found guilty.' I'm not going to tie myself into an impossible situation. Under promise, over deliver has always been my mantra.

'Quite so,' said the general. 'In this case; I expect a tourist will not be found guilty then. Nice to drop in on you, Cyril.' He leaves the room with such force that papers on the desk take flight like white egrets and flutter to the floor.

I turn to Cyril, who pushes over a case file. Opening the thin folder, I can see it is marked "Closed". It has the picture taken from the ID card of Leap Son. A short extract explains that he was a peasant who died of natural causes whilst travelling from Battambang to Siem Reap for business on the Angkor Express bus. In the commentary, it noted that

"Reports that he had been stabbed were confused with the fact that he was carrying a Khmer ceremonial knife."

'Sign it off, Michael as Chief Inspector. I will then stamp and countersign it,' Cyril said in a no-nonsense, resigned manner. He ended with a huge sigh.

'But sir. This is not true.'

'Come now Chief Inspector Suon, since when has truth been important in Cambodia?' He nearly manages to keep a straight face.

I don't rise to it. I understand Cyril is frustrated by the Cambodian system and has tried to improve the quality of justice in the area. It is a pretty soul-destroying effort as he is being constantly undermined from above.

'Possibly more important,' he says, 'was the speed that our general heard of this incident and the fact that it is so important for him to make a personal visit. Who is this dead "peasant"?'

'Well, young Private Cheng had the ID card. I will have to look into him; apart from that, the only person was Sergeant Munny. I've known him for years. I've also tasked Munny with getting the body to the morgue. Do you think we need to get the body moved somewhere safe until we know what is going on here?' Cyril and I don't like being interfered with by the military.

'OK, you get hold of Munny and ask him where the body is.' Cyril is as suspicious of all our staff as I am.

I ring Munny on his mobile, 'Have you got the body to the morgue yet?'

'I'm still waiting for the CSI team to arrive, sir.'

'The police chief and I have decided that getting the statements right is more important, so go and make sure

Cheng is doing a good job. I will get the CSI guys to bring the body in.'

'Are you sure, sir? It is important that we don't lose this body.'

Cyril listens as I have the phone loudspeaker on. He gives the thumbs down sign.

'Well, we are more concerned with handling the foreigners correctly and you are my sergeant; that's an order.'

'OK sir, but I could probably do both.'

'Thanks for the offer Sergeant, leave it to the CSI guys and make sure you supervise Cheng personally.'

Turning to Cyril, I say, 'I guess that puts our number one suspect for the spy as Munny. I will make some checks on Cheng if you can manage the body, sir?'

Cyril rings his contact in the coroner's office. 'All done. I am taking the body out of the system for a while. We will get another corpse sent to the morgue in its place.' There is always some drunk peasant lying around. 'You, my friend, are going to have to be a real detective now.' Then, counting off on his fingers, 'I want to understand who this dead man is, why anyone would want to kill him and who did. I don't want our general to know what we are doing, so you need to find who you can trust. Obviously not your sergeant. Finally, I want you to tell me how we can use all this information to get our department some respect from our corrupt commanders!' He has run out of fingers and is now banging on the desk.

'Another day in the paradise our Kingdom is,' I shout back as I leave the room with Cyril laughing in the background.

Trawling through the personnel files in the basement, I can't find anything to link Sergeant Munny and the military, and he has been working for me for the last five years. Unfortunately, in Cambodia, loyalty is an easily bought commodity.

As for Cheng, from his files, he seems as clean as can be. He was an orphan who had grown up in a monastery, which is unremarkable. An outstanding student, he had exceptional scores in all the tests, but without sponsors, he was destined to stay at a low rank. At eighteen, he had left the monkhood and joined the local police. The force is like the Buddhist brotherhood; without sponsorship you would not be going far. This is how things are; you need connections to make your way. Could the general be Cheng's path to advancement? I dig deep but can't find any opportunity for the pair to meet.

I have taken to Cheng today. He seems a really bright lad, the sort I can mould into a detective, far more than Munny. After a good time checking, I make my decision. Cheng is not a military spy, well, not yet. He is a ripe young fruit ready to be picked. Closing the files, it is eight pm, far too late. My home is only a short walk across the river into the old quarter, where my father-in-law, Prak Suk, has bought my family a lovely flat. Prak is my sponsor; he helps my career run smoothly through the bureaucratic cabal that runs our country. He has a network of "friends" who run the region's power system, and nothing electrical gets connected without his say-so. His connections mean we also get free power to go with our modern flat.

Arriving home, my wife, Bophra scolds me for being late. She fully understands the pressures I have at work, but admonishing a late returning husband is a mandatory response for any traditional Cambodian mother. My children come hurtling to me to tell me about their adventures of the day.

With that and food I am occupied until bedtime when I can ask Bophra about her day.

'It is hard at school for Jimmy,' she sobs gently into my chest.

Jimmy is my boy, named after Jimmy Osmond, who sang Bophra's favourite song *Long-haired Lover from Liverpool.* Somewhere in pregnancy, it all went wrong for Jimmy. He was born a gorgeous bundle of joy but with Down's Syndrome.

Education is poor in Siem Reap; the provision for disabled children is pitiful. Poor Bophra has to take the brunt of the comments from the other wives about why we kept him. As if we had a choice! And then from the teachers who say to leave him at home as school can't help him. I sometimes stay late at work just to avoid the remorseful apologising that Bophra lavishes on me. She blames herself totally for his condition. I cannot help but unconditionally love my little boy, who is the Sun and Earth, to me. I despair for the grief it gives her.

Bophra looks cross with me as my phone rings. A text from Cyril, "Body safe at the other morgue". We have a less official place for our more discreet investigations, not everything needs to be open to the glare of public scrutiny or for that fact all the officers in the police department. "Meet me there at seven *AM,* don't tell your sergeant." So, I assume from this that our mole is Sergeant Munny after all.

The "Other" Morgue

Our second morgue is hidden in the lower level of the hospital and known only to Cyril, myself, Dr Pang, our pathologist and a couple of old technicians, who understand the need for secrecy.

'So,' says Cyril, 'what killed him?' No doubt he has been up since five AM. After all, he is a country boy; however, Cyril is often irritable this early before the good coffee is available.

'Good question,' replies Pang. 'Palpably not the knife. That was stuck in a long time after death, hence the lack of blood.'

'So it was the cord?' I ask.

'Possibly,' says Pang mysteriously, 'but then again.'

'How else could he have fucking died?' shouts Cyril, starting to turn puce. Sometimes he is more than irritable; he needs that coffee.

'There is a strange puncture wound in his neck that was potentially made whilst he was still alive. I don't know what caused that and what damage it did. I will need to have a full autopsy and send samples away to test. Remember, I haven't had a chance to open him up yet!'

'But he could have been strangled?' I pursue, as I think the French women are such obvious perpetrators.

'He certainly has blue around his mouth showing signs of oxygen deprivation, but so many things can cause that.'

'OK, so how old is he, and where is he from?' asks Cyril tersely.

'I would think those questions are more in your field than mine. At a guess, let's put him in his sixties. By the number of healed wounds he has, I would suggest he has led a very violent past.'

'Khmer Rouge?' I ask.

'Fuck, fuck, fuck,' swears Cyril. 'Who the fuck is he?' Everything about our tragic past and the villains who caused so many deaths enrages him.

'I think, boss, you will have to use your contacts to find that out. By the way, I assume that you proved Munny was certainly the mole?'

'Yes, the bloody rat; he was sneaking around trying to find out if we had switched the bodies, a bit too interested for my liking. So I sent him away, down to Battambang last night to investigate the tourists' movements there.'

'An expense account and a few days out of town and I'm sure he will stay out of our hair!' I agree. 'OK, so today I will interview the foreigners starting with the French women sitting directly behind the victim, Leap Son. Doctor, if you find any forensics, please ring me.' With that, I bid them farewell and set off to meet Private Cheng at the Ta Prohm Hotel. I didn't want to interview the ladies at the station, in case Munny had some colleagues there. I have already sent a note to Cheng and had had him reassigned to me from general duties; I need a sharp young man. I just hope that the ladies speak English as my French is appalling.

The Ta Prohm is a traditional, four-star tourist hotel, swathed in wood and carvings with highly attentive staff. Cheng had asked the Cambodian manager for a room, to which he obliged in an instant. It is always good for hotel managers to keep onside with the police.

Jasmine and Lavande Hough, spinsters of Orleans, France, aged forty-five and forty-seven, sit before me in the bed-cum-interview room. Cheng stands by the door in what I hope is a menacing position. I have arranged for two plastic water bottles in front of the ladies and have turned the air-con off. I'm sure these two Europeans will start to suffer before Cheng and I notice the heat.

Their passports are both fresh. This seems to be their first trip since they were issued only a couple of months ago. Are they novice travellers or experienced assassins who travel on counterfeit papers? At first glance, they're not the most obvious killers. They are both short with time turning their once slimmish figures to middle-aged fat. They have a hint of Cambodian in their features. This may well be important.

Both have light, well-groomed hair and smart travel clothes which are chic and look comfortable. Each is armed with a handbag of intimidating size. Neither seems to smoke as I had made sure Cheng had searched both their purses and rooms. They smell of scents far more subtle than their names portray.

Being a country with a one-party state and a history for murder and conflict, everyone assumes that we have a secret police force and all the accoutrements of a Soviet-style Big Brother system to feed it with information. We may well have.

I am as much in the dark about it as any common citizen. As my investigation is strictly off the books due to the general's instructions, I have no access to the ladies' prior travel history. I will bluff.

'So ladies, can we do this in English, or do you need an interpreter?' I start brightly to counter my earlier tough image. I plan on accusing them of murder, but you can't start at that level of venom. I am a great believer in boiling the frog.

'We could speak in Cambodian if you wish,' answers Jasmine. I note that Jasmine is wearing white whilst Lavande, her sister, wears purple. So convenient of them.

'You speak Cambodian?' I ask in Cambodian.

'Enough to get by,' she answers back with a very formal accent. She hasn't lived here, that is for sure.

'Please,' says Lavande, who has already started to develop beads of sweat on her temple. 'My sister can speak, but I am a poor linguist, so can we compromise on English?'

There are tensions here between the two of them, which may be useful. But first to the new passports. It is probably worth digging into their travel history, especially with Jasmine's language fluency. Leaving them to stew, I text a friend in the immigration office. I know his sister has been waiting a while for a power connection. I intend to solve her electricity problem in exchange for some travel information. Using my father-in-law's position helps me outperform other officers in the department. This process takes some time. The ladies shuffle uncomfortably and perspire more profusely.

I find "waiting" a really useful tool in interviewing, so after I finish my text, I check the progress of the dragon races in Phnom Penh. I'm not betting on them; it is just a convenient subject to distract me whilst they simmer.

'Have you come to ask us something or to read your bloody phone?' By her tone, I have already wound Jasmine up.

I finish checking on the races. They don't begin until later and even I, a keen race buff, find the punditry dull.

'Have you anything you wish to tell me, ladies?' I pick up my pen and pad, ready to take notes.

Lavande starts to speak but is shoved in the ribs by the older Jasmine.

'Do I have to talk to you separately?' I smile.

Jasmine's make up is starting to bubble in the heat of the room as she looks at her sister and says, 'We wish to have a lawyer.'

'I am sure you will need one, Ms Hough,' I have been practising my English and love the word Ms to signify neither Mrs nor Miss. 'It's just that you don't get access to one until I've finished with you here, we are not in Paris.'

'I am Madam Hough,' Jasmine interrupts me with a shower of light, unintended spittle. She covers her mouth too late to cover her *faux pas*.

'So sorry,' I answer, ignoring the droplets of saliva on my notebook. Bloody French! There goes my "Ms" whimsy. Looking directly at Jasmine, I ask, 'First Madam Hough, you will tell me why you were on the bus from Battambang to Siem Reap.' I try to look concerned as I leaf through a bough envelope full of papers. The sheets have nothing to do with this interview. I am though trying to imply that they have some significance in my questions.

To my surprise, Lavande starts to weep. Her sister holds her hand and soothes her in French, then she turns to me. I keep still, this is a time to listen.

'We were both born in Phnom Penh, Monsieur. Our father was a doctor at the hospital. We lived through the bombings of the Khmer Rouge and were taken in by the embassy when the city fell. Our mother was a Cambodian, so she was given up by the embassy.'

'Given up?'

'Surely you know your own history, Chief Inspector? The Khmer Rouge killed everyone who had collaborated with a foreigner. The embassy staff gave our mother away to be murdered, to save their own miserable lives.'

'Ah yes, so sorry, please do continue,' I have tried to forget the hideous events of the Khmer Rouge; rarely is it brought back so fresh and personal.

'We were kept alive by Mrs Hough. Her husband had died trying to help other French citizens reach the embassy. She got us on the transports out when they finally came. Of course, we were only very small. My sister was six months old; I was two and a half.'

This story seems to have nothing to do with the murder but certainly connects the ladies with Cambodia in a way that is far more than that of a tourist trip.

'We were told that our father worked for the Khmer for months at the hospital until he finally became too weak. No one knows when or where he died. The commander of the hospital was called Colonel Son Leap. None of the Western doctors or nurses survived, despite saving thousands of Khmer soldiers. We were told Son Leap would kill one of the medical staff every time one of his soldiers died. He continued until there were no staff left.'

I hadn't heard this story. It could, of course, be a lie from the Vietnamese or propaganda from France. But among the other brutalities inflicted by the Khmer Rouge, it is hard to tell.

Jasmine lapses into silence, having gushed out her story. It hasn't taken us any further. What is this all about?

'And your trip on the bus, Madam?' Curiously, "Madam" does suit this situation better.

'And Monsieur, I have spent my entire life tracking down that bastard Colonel Son Leap!' she shouts back at me, unexpected spittle again spraying as she shouts. The veins on her neck are pulsing and her cheeks are showing bright red through her heavy makeup.

'And we killed him,' adds Lavande in a small whimper.

They both fall into floods of tears and hug each other. I half expect them to start a sterling rendition of the *Marseillaise*.

'Yes, we killed the bastard who murdered our father, and we don't regret it, and we will tell the world what we have done. Your filthy, corrupt government is still hiding many murderous butchers like him who should have been brought to justice!' Jasmine spits out passionately.

The ferocity of her language is genuinely shocking. Of course, I have heard rumours of ex Khmer Rouge officers reintegrating into society, especially in the security services where they were fighting the hated Vietnamese. I haven't heard of Colonel Son Leap and doubt that our Leap Son is the same man. Cambodia is full of people called Son; it is a very popular name, analogous to Smith, Jones, Wang or Li. How can these women possibly know that these two "Sons" are the same person? And be so certain that they could murder him in such a personal fashion. They must have known that they were bound to be caught?

I have no other options; I have confessed killers on my hands.

'Ladies, I am afraid that following your confession I must arrest you for the murder of Leap Son yesterday on the Angkor Express.' I turn to Cheng and tell him to cuff them and take them to the central police station; texting Cyril with a quick update, "The shit is going to hit the fan now!"

The American

Although the case looks closed, I do want to know where the knife came from and understand who would stick it into a corpse? Working outwards from Leap Son's body, the next closest person in the bus is the young brash American, twenty-six-year-old David Smith, another suspiciously common name. He has been told to stay at his backpackers' hostel which is close to Pub Street, the party area of Siem Reap, and only a stone's throw from the Ta Prohm.

Leaving Cheng, I feel comfortable that I can handle this one alone. David is on the roof terrace. He looks like he is recovering from a heavy night on the town. There are a couple of Angkor beer cans and an overfull ashtray on the low table, whilst he, most ignorantly, has his bare feet on the opposite chair. Not a knowledgeable traveller then. Looking at his passport it is full of trips between Thailand, Cambodia, and Vietnam. His entry documents state his occupation as a student and his residency as Racine, Wisconsin, USA.

'Good morning Mr Smith, do you mind?' I point to the seat where his feet are.

'Oh, sorry.' As far as American accents go, his was pretty clear with no local drawl, so an educated man?

'A long way from home, Mr Smith?' I always try to be polite.

'I like the Far East; it's cooler than home in summer and warmer than home in winter.' He oozes confidence, I am sure this, along with an athletic frame and long blond hair makes him a winner with the ladies. His youth is emphasised by the ubiquitous American baseball cap.

'And how do you pay for all this leisure travelling?' The first flicker of doubt crosses his face. I am not concerned with this interview, but it seems I may have hit a little sore spot.

'What has that got to do with yesterday?' he retorts a bit testily before recovering. 'I've got plenty of dough. My family is loaded.' He seems to speak with a mixture of pride and regret. A conflicted youth?

I study my notes, which have nothing to do with this case. I just want to leave this question in the air. Will he give me more or has he recovered his composure? If I blag now and get it wrong, I will lose and learn nothing. As he isn't the murderer, it hardly matters, so I just plough on. 'That's not exactly what we have on record here.'

I see a flash of panic as his eyes dilate. Looking down to the ground, he says, 'Look, I know I was a bit short of cash when I came in, but that was due to a card getting cancelled in error. I'm good to stay in Cambodia for another couple of weeks, then I'm off back to Thailand.'

As he is rattled, I ask the question I desperately want an answer to. 'Where is the knife you bought in Battambang?'

Sergeant Munny had come up trumps for me here. He had texted that a local knife trader had been keen to help him by identifying the big blond American who had bought a large Khmer knife. Munny must have traipsed around all the dealers to get this information. He must know that he is in the doghouse.

A line of perspiration breaks out on David's brow and slowly slides into his eye. He wipes it away with the back of his hand. Looking up at me, he says, 'Am I under caution? I didn't hear you read me my rights?'

The second Westerner convinced that we have to follow their rules. 'We don't have to do that sort of thing here, Mr Smith; people are either innocent or guilty. My job is to find out which. You can argue your case if it gets to court, otherwise, I suggest you answer me honestly. Where is the ten cm bladed knife you bought in Battambang market yesterday morning before you got on the Angkor Express where an innocent Cambodian man died?'

'Innocent, my arse!' He laughs loudly. 'That bastard was a two-timing, double-crossing drugs dealer, who would sell his daughter for a profit.'

'So, you knew Leap Son?' I think I'll pursue the knife later.

'I don't know about his name, but I am sure about who he was. I've tracked him from the Thai border.'

'To kill him?' I ask.

'You'll have to find that out in front of a judge, I'm not saying any more until I see the US Consulate.' With that, he folds his arms and sinks down into a ball on his seat, pulling his legs towards his chest like an upset child.

Arresting the Hough sisters is going to cause waves, taking in this young American will be more than even Cyril can handle. Drug smuggling is not a crime I usually investigate, nor normally are foreigners, unless it is a criminal case like murder, so I take the most prudent action.

'Mr Smith, I will leave the consulate up to you. I insist you stay in this hostel until we say otherwise.' I stand up and look down at him in my most officious pose. 'We don't kill our criminals here as you do in the USA, but I assure you our prisons are very unpleasant. You would do best to come clean now.'

As I see another text from Cyril to return to the office flash across my phone screen, I get up and leave the young American curled up and astonishingly sucking his thumb.

I expect my boss is ducking shit back at the station. I text the duty sergeant to assign a couple of boys to keep an eye on the American. There seems to be plenty of opportunities for overtime with this case, which will please everyone, except Cyril.

Whilst walking back, I try to work out how I keep the arrest of two middle-aged French tourists who are screaming about the Khmer Rouge and our implicit government out of the press. This is such a big story now and unfortunately, the massed international press are crawling around town hunting for scoops. They have all been attracted by our opposition leader, who has called for a revolution and is threatening to appear from his exile in Paris. I believe even the general cannot hold me to account if this gets picked up by a journalist.

To my surprise, as I arrive back at the station, there is a demonstration. Could the Houghs have organised this? What the hell is going on? Slipping in by the side door, I use my personal key; it's a private entrance and a useful way of avoiding enquiring eyes, and often irate wives. I go up the stairs and into Cyril's office, where he has the general and a number of other inspectors from around the region.

The general sees me. 'What the fuck have you been doing, Suon?'

As this is such a broad question, I decide to stall rather than step into a bear trap. 'I have just arrived, General. What are you referring to?'

'These bloody animal rights people. What have you been doing?' He is barking out words like a howler monkey. Genuinely confused, and much relieved that this has nothing to do with me, I smile as he continues. 'I told you your Angkor Express case was closed; now we have a riot by the doors of the police station.'

'But I don't understand the link General, this has nothing to do with me.' I open my arms and palms in an effort to show complete innocence. Rule number one in the police is never lie when you don't need to.

Cyril stands up behind his desk, to his full commanding height of one hundred and sixty centimetres. 'General, we have a situation here, let's not squabble. The Chief Inspector seems as confused as I am as to how this came about. Who has been to see these Dutch tourists?'

'Sir, I haven't seen them since we released everybody yesterday on the general's instructions.' I am in full supplicant mode. 'What has happened?'

'Well, the two Dutch passengers came in about a half an hour ago, surrounded by the crowd you see outside. They say that they have killed the man on the Angkor Express because he is a dog murderer.' Cyril calmly explains. 'I have been told by some of my younger and more tech-savvy detectives that the demonstration outside is being streamed on the internet with thousands of "hits" and that the couple have posted a full confession explaining why they killed Leap Son on the bus yesterday. If this is a slow day with global news, we could soon all be on CNN!'

The press who I thought would be my saviour may now sink me. Hopefully, Sam Rainsy, our erstwhile subversive leader, will start the revolution and get everybody off my back. He had promised the world that he would arrive through Thailand and overcome the current government. Everybody is afraid, and the world's media are circling like vultures over a dying man in the desert. It's not nice being seen as a ravaged corpse by the world's press, again.

'We must suppress the demonstration,' shouts the general, bringing the comments of the Hough sisters about the remnants of the Khmer Rouge being a part of our present-day command structure right to my mind.

'I have neither the manpower for that General, nor the expertise in my men,' Cyril counters.

'We must shut off the internet,' the general continues. 'The Iranians have done it, the Vietnamese have shut off the BBC, get it done!'

'Again, General, you are in a local police station. We don't have such resources here. I will do my best to close the road and push the protesters into the corner across the street. Any more needs to be done by your men.' Cyril is talking quietly and slowly, his arms out wide and palms splayed; he has been to the same crowd control training course as I have.

'I can't be involved; I can't be seen to be here. Don't you understand how delicate the situation is at the moment? We are on a precipice, over the edge is a return to the chaos of the past. We have been fighting outside intervention, political rivals, gangsters, the Vietnamese, and the French just to maintain control. Do you want the old days back?' The general is fuming, waving his hands around like a whomping willow.

In all honesty, I am confused as to which "old days" he is referring to. Our country has such a chequered past. The only reason most of us don't want to have a change now is that all the past revolutions have merely made life worse. The most common reaction to a proposed uprising in Cambodia is "Can you promise it will be better after?" Obama may think it is all about "change". Here we are more with Trump. We only want things better, and if that means putting up with the general, censorship, lack of freedom, corruption, the Chinese and the King, then so be it.

'Why were you here, General?' I ask as he must have arrived before the Dutch couple.

'I heard you found where the Son Leap murder weapon came from. I thought I had told you to close the investigation?' Answering questions seems to make the general calmer.

I wonder if that is a slip of the tongue. Should I check if he meant Leap Son? Or does he know more, and does this back up the Houghs' identification?

Whilst we are talking, Cyril leaves to organise moving the protesters back.

'The police chief sent my sergeant to Battambang to understand what had happened there, just tying up loose ends.' I haven't asked how the general had found out. His lack of discretion shows he doesn't care that I know he has a man in our team. 'What do you want me to do now?'

'You are going to have to be very careful, Chief Inspector Suon. You will also have to learn to follow the chain of command and follow orders. Your father-in-law may have a good position now, but he could lose it, do you understand?' I nod. In Cambodia, we all understand how it is.

'You want me to find the truth about Leap Son?' I ask meekly, looking for a change in his expression.

'I want you to find a way to exonerate every foreigner on that bus, whether they want it or not, to keep the press away from the truth and to leave Leap Son as a rice trader who simply died. Can you do that, Suon? Can I trust you?'

I am tall for a Cambodian and look down at the general by a full head. He is still a terrifying presence, muscled like a bulldog, with a thick neck and sweaty shiny skin.

'I will find out the truth and report to you sir, what you do with that is not my concern. I will not communicate with the press as ever. Finding out who Leap Son is has never been the purpose of my murder investigation. I will keep anything I find about him out of the report unless pertinent. Will that do, General?'

He huffs, 'That will have to do. Now get me out of here without being seen. I'm currently too fat to be on "YouTube".' His laugh is scary. Following his previous threats, I wonder how sane our political and military leaders are.

As the general leaves, Cyril, who has returned from organising the troops, says, 'A Faustian pact with the general, Michael? Let's hope you manage to save your soul.'

Dogmeat

Outside, the boys are managing the foreign mob commendably well. They have pushed them back gently, on to a corner plot which we leave free for such small demonstrations. The beauty of this is that the trees break up the protestors, making their numbers look far lower and the opportunity for concerted chanting more difficult. We tell them that in the shade they will be more comfortable. Then we use our new Chinese imported face recognition software to ensure that none of these people are ever allowed visas again. The local police charge the vendors an extra "fee" for selling drinks nearby, anything to help a poor policeman.

I call over a young private to get me a pamphlet, then go inside to watch the confession on my laptop and read.

Cambodian Friends

STOP THE TORTURE OF MILLIONS OF DOGS AND CATS BE A VOICE FOR THE VOICELESS. WOULD YOU EAT YOUR PET?
PETS ARE STOLEN TO FEED THE DOG AND CAT MEAT TRADE
20% OF STRAY DOGS HAVE RABIES

THIS MEAT IS NOT CAMBODIAN CULTURE
100 PEOPLE DIED LAST YEAR EATING INFECTED MEAT

Join Us and Fight for Animal Rights
www.Petsarenotmeat.com

There are associated pictures and stories. This is a health risk that I have read about before. I can understand why people ate dog meat in the dark days of the war, but there is no need to now. I'm sure if I was a young Cambodian student, I would be standing beside the protesters, if for no other reason than public health. With this positive attitude, I watch the confession tape.

Karol and Isabella are both thirty-four-year-old Dutch students, although of what is not clear as surely they are getting on a bit.

Video Clip (Spoken Jointly)

'We contacted Leap Son with the pretence of opening a new restaurant in Singapore and told him we needed a regular supply of dog meat. He promised us that he could supply twenty dogs a week, and he arranged to meet us at his slaughterhouse in Siem Reap.

Online, he had shown us videos of dead dogs, which he had skinned and then frozen. He was also going to show us the meat container, which we could transport right through Thailand and Malaysia. He told us he knew many day-trippers who would smuggle the dogs through in chiller boxes across the Singapore border.

We had become so revolted by the pictures he had sent us, which are now posted on the animal rights website *www.Petsarenotmeat.com,* that we decided to confront him. We realised he was on the bus as we waited to board and approached him. He just laughed and spat on the ground, then pointed to a mangy dog by the road and said "YUMYUM".

At the final rest stop an hour outside, Siem Reap we decided he just didn't deserve to live. That not another animal would die for his greed. So, we took a knife from the restaurant and stabbed him as we went past his seat. Putting a hand over his mouth, we both pushed in the blade. He silently slumped against the window.

We murdered him like he had killed so many defenceless dogs. We are martyrs to the cause of animal protection. Please join us to fight this horrible trade, both here in Cambodia and all over the world.

Please contact us on *www.Petsarenotmeat.com and fund us now.* '

VIDEO ENDS with horrendous pictures of dead and mutilated cats and dogs.

Their story is so full of holes it is-laughable. They know they are not murderers; they are just using us as a publicity stunt. How all the other rights activists have accumulated here without us knowing in advance is another mystery, but luckily for me that one will definitively land on Samnang's desk. One thing I will give to Leap Son, he seems to be the ideal Cambodian entrepreneur with fingers in every pie.

I have almost forgotten my two real suspects; neither Cyril nor the general mentioned the fact that there are two foreigners in our cells already. Maybe these animal lovers have done me a favour. Duty calls. I will check on the sisters before I interrogate the Dutch pair. I promised the general I would finish the investigation, then turn it over to him to prosecute. If he wants to let the sisters free, then who am I?

My phone flashes a message from my wife. "I'm at the hospital. Jimmy is in Ward 10."

I brief Cheng, who is in the locker room, check on the French ladies with the custody officer, then send a brief text to Cyril to explain. He loves my kids and is their favourite uncle, so he would back me in family versus work every time. I am just starting to spin too many plates.

As I run to the hospital a million things go through my mind, Jimmy is so susceptible to illness, bullying, accidents, and general life. I crash through the ward doors; they all know me well from my many visits.

'Chief Inspector,' the improbably clean and smart ward matron comes to me.

'What's wrong, matron?'

'It's his stomach this time. I think he's eaten something poisonous. He's convulsing and going into seizures, not normal behaviour even for Jimmy.' She has cared for him as much as we have and is practically his second mum.

I go to his bed where my wife is sitting crying. I try to comfort her, but she won't look me in the eye. Her family is far more traditional than my own, despite her father being a big cheese. His power base is from the rural areas around the mountains and coast to the south.

'What is it, dear? I'm sure he'll be OK. They've pumped his stomach now, so he should be fine.'

She still looks the other way and sobs. I have a terrible feeling. 'Have you been giving him something?' She is a village girl, after all, and I have often had to stop her from giving the children rustic remedies.

'The ladies said it would cure him, that it is an old remedy.'

'What have you given him? You need to tell the nurse right now so they can ask the doctor.'

'I think it was dog meat,' she whimpers.

'Fucking dog meat!' I jump up and shout. All the ward turns to look at me. 'What possessed you? You stupid woman!' I know I am protesting too much, but the last thing my poor boy needs is to be poisoned by some foul, pest-infested mongrel prepared by a village shaman. The pictures from the animal rights website flash through my mind.

I go over to the matron and explain what my wife has done. 'What will happen, sister?'

'Well, it could be a number of things, but the only ones with these symptoms are rabies or, in the worst case, a neurotoxin poison, which they use to kill the dogs. The only help for that would be the stomach pump and we've done that. I will call the doctor now. I'm afraid rabies jabs aren't covered under healthcare. You will have to pay for that and it's two hundred dollars.'

'Do you think I care about the money? This is my son. He is priceless.' The matron blushes; she understands how much we have spent on Jimmy, but she still has to make sure we will pay.

'I'm sorry,' I said, ashamed at my tone with her, 'I'm just a bit upset.'

'Don't worry, Chief Inspector, we will do everything.' As ever, she is all professional. She would have made a far better wife than Bophra. As a Christian, it isn't my way just to jump ship, so to speak, though I often think about it.

Bophra and I sit, not speaking for the next four hours, whilst the doctors fill my poor boy with no end of drugs. At midnight, he appears to turn a corner. Looking at my lovely wife, I tell her I am sorry and that I know she only did it because she loves Jimmy. Then I repeat that if she ever gives him anything not prescribed by the doctor or eaten by me, she would not be forgiven again.

'But you don't like jelly, Daddy,' Jimmy mumbles his first words since coming into the hospital.

'OK, Jimmy, we will make an exception for jelly,' I reply tearfully.

I text the good news to Cyril, then go home to bed. I have a lot of catch up to do tomorrow.

More Murder

Getting into the office at six am is not normally so difficult. With Bophra still in the hospital watching Jimmy, I'm now looking after Jenny. Today is a national holiday, the second day of Dragon boat racing. I had intended to take the kids to the races in town, as there are street markets and games everywhere and neither are old enough yet to be in their school's Dragon boat teams. A policeman's lot is evidently not a happy one. So, Jenny is sitting at the end of my desk, casually reading the witness statements from the Angkor Express investigation.

'Did the French ladies kill him then, Daddy?' she asks, her eyes wide open. 'They must be really mean.'

I splutter into my iced coffee, 'Put those down! They are confidential.'

'Oh come on, you tell Mummy everything that happens at work.'

I have a sudden horrific thought that Jenny has been passing on to her friends at school, all the intelligence gathered by me during my investigations. I shudder, 'You don't tell anyone, do you?'

'Oh no daddy, mummy says we are to keep everything you say a secret. She only tells grandad.'

Hmm, that figures, the old goat likes to be well informed and honestly, he has helped me so much this may be the best way to repay him. Plausible deniability, the Americans would call it.

'I am off to find the answer to your question right now, darling, so you be good. Put those witness statements down and read your Harry Potter.'

Cheng is waiting for me in the interview room. He has made sure the two ladies have been separated for the last twenty-four hours, which was a great move. He really shows promise. I would be so disappointed if it turned out he was in the general's pay.

I decide to talk to Lavande first, as she seems the weaker of the two, but Cyril interrupts me. 'Sorry, Michael, we have another couple of deaths.'

'Cyril, this is Siem Reap, not Baltimore or St. Louis. What do you mean, another two murders?'

'Two locals have been found mutilated.'

'Well, don't you have other detectives?' I ask sarcastically.

'Yes, I do. It just so happens that the two dead bodies are probably the two locals on your Angkor Express interested?'

How can I not be? 'Where were they found?'

'You won't believe this, but in Ta Prohm temple.'

'In the Angkor Wat complex? Shit, this will be all over the news.'

'No, it won't. I've had the Ta Prohm temple complex sealed for "safety concerns". I'll keep it closed until tomorrow. That should give you enough time to investigate if you go now.'

I rush upstairs to get the witness statements. How this couple could be involved with Leap Son is a complete blank to me. They couldn't have been killed by the French ladies, the American we have been watching and the Dutch are incarcerated in the station. So, who did that leave and why would anyone else be involved? I find Jenny pretending to read her book. She has the files of witness statements poking out above the cover sleeve.

'OK, then Jenny, who else apart from the American, Dutch animal rights protesters and the French women were on the bus?'

Jenny's face lights up. 'Am I on your team?'

'Just help me do this quickly.'

'Well, there was the mystery local couple in the back seats.'

'They are no longer a mystery. I'm just going to inspect their bodies in Angkor Wat.'

She looks at me, horrified. 'How can you be so casual, dad?'

Possibly I shouldn't expect a twelve-year-old to be as jaundiced about life as myself.

'I suppose this is what your job is actually like. Wow!' She brushes herself down as her mother would do in a crisis. 'OK, so who do we have left? Kiry and Pich, the Vietnamese newlyweds on their honeymoon to the temples: Robert and Ellen, the middle-aged English; Florin and Sofia, the Romanians, and finally Loren and Denise, the French couple. The French seem a bit strange, dad. Private Cheng notes that they know way too much about Cambodia for mere tourists.'

'Thank you, darling, leave the sleuthing to me. Give me those official reports now and wait here until I get back. Just ask Cheng to get you something if you are hungry.' With that, I hustle downstairs, appropriate a moped, and drive to Angkor Wat, a fifteen-minute hop out of town.

Is it a coincidence that I interviewed Jasmine and Lavande at the Ta Prohm Hotel, and now at the temple that it's named after our two errant Cambodian travellers turn up? As soon as I arrive, I see Dr Pang coming out.

'I haven't had them on the slab yet.' He snaps before I can say a word. He sounds pretty testy. 'The only reason we know who they are is that they kept the bus tickets from yesterday, probably needed them to claim expenses.'

'What's wrong Sonith?' It was ironic that a man whose name meant soft and gentle could be so hard and cranky.

'No one has any respect anymore. How could you murder someone in such a sacred place? You know these are religious sites, not just tourist traps.' He turns and bows owards the temple as he leaves.

Switching the conversation back to the pair, I ask, 'Not a suicide pact made by frustrated peasants, then?' Tragically, youngsters frustrated by the lack of opportunity commonly kill themselves in outlandish ways to have their moment of fame.

'Go see for yourself; they were neither frustrated nor peasants. I couldn't tell you if they felt suicidal. They drip with expensive Western jewellery and the smell of real Chanel perfume. What was such a rich young pair doing on a tourist bus?' he arches his eyebrows.

'Surely those are questions I should be asking, Doctor, but thanks for the hints and I bow to your knowledge of expensive perfumes,' I answer jovially. 'You couldn't just tell me how they died?'

My attempts to lighten his spirits are falling on deaf ears. 'I haven't had the test results, but I would suggest they have both died from haemorrhagic shock following massive and rapid exsanguination whilst under the influence of heroin. I know the signs.' He tapped his forehead. 'As for the perfume, it just so happens that it is my wife's favourite, and I promise you it is expensive and difficult to procure.'

'So, suicide then?'

'It's very difficult to commit suicide by injecting yourself whilst your hands and feet are tied together! This looks more like a brutal interrogation, which entailed the removal of skin, slice by slice. I don't know whether this killed them first or if, in fact, the drugs got them. I will only possibly know after a postmortem. Whoever did this was a nasty son of a bitch, and I want you to catch him, Michael.'

'A him?'

'Again, that's your job, just look for a nasty vicious bastard who enjoys inflicting pain.'

As he rushes off, I turn to enter the temple made famous by the Lara Croft film. This case seems to have more than a touch in common with a big Hollywood production, though it looks like a low-cost slasher film.

The bodies are both wrapped around the famous trees which have grown over and into the temple like giant Ents from the *Lord of the Rings*. Their smart clothes have been cut in strips by a sharp blade, and they have bled into the ground below. This is going to take some effort for the temple staff to clean up. I realise that I haven't asked the doctor for a time of death. It must have been after the park closed at 5.30 pm, and before the bodies were discovered by the early staff at

5.00 am. Nearly a twelve-hour window without a soul about no likelihood of a witness then.

There are liaison guys on site who tell me that they will be going through the CCTV. We are trying to be modern here at Angkor, but there is so much land to cover it is impossible to video everywhere. Last night, most of the staff tell me that they were in town celebrating after the first day of the dragon races.

With the forensics team taking photographs and a small group outfitted in white paper onesies looking for evidence, there is little more I can glean from the site. At the edge of the temple, I see a simple bamboo mat.

'Hey you!' I call over the security guard, 'Whose mat is that?'

'It's just a mad old woman who professes to be a female monk or some such nonsense. She lives around the temples, scrounging tourist donations.'

'And what did she tell you?'

'Well, er, no one talks to her. She's a bit crazy, sir, lives in the ruins and all.'

'Find her and bring her to me. I'll be reading reports on my moped.'

The old hag is brought shuffling along to me. She puts out her hands in deference, then winks, the cheeky act of a sly old lady who knows how to twist the world to her bidding. I smile at her, 'So, you live here?'

'Yes, for the sake of the gods,' she mumbles back. She sounds a hundred years old and the crags in her face suggest many years in the harsh sun. I guess she is not much more than seventy-five, old enough to have lived through the dark days.

'Did you see anything, or hear anything last night?' As I mention "hear" she shudders. 'What did you hear?'

'There was pain and screaming, sir, like in the old times.' By her tense shoulders, I see that this has disturbed her. As I had guessed, the "old times" is a reference to when the complex was in the hands of the Khmer Rouge.

'And what did you see?' I look deeply into her eyes. I glare at her, full of self-belief. She must submit to my will. We stand locked together in our duel of egos. I am always going to be the victor.

'There was a car and a large man dressed in Western clothes, but it was dark,' She lets out a breath and sags in defeat.

'Where?' I ask. The area has been covered by a horde of police and guards this morning, but you never know your luck. She points to the car park, which is tarmacked. We walk over. I can definitely see some drag marks, the back of a shoe perhaps? I will get the forensics team to check. 'And?' I look at her again.

Now her eyes have gone blank. She is not going to respond further.

A large man? Well, that would exclude the newlyweds. I doubt anyone would call Kiry large, nor would you describe Florin Stoica large, but the Frenchman and Englishman, either of them could fit the bill. My interrogation list is getting longer now. I will have to have both men brought in. So much for keeping foreigners away from the station. This afternoon there will be six of them there. We could run out of room, so I need to clear some more suspects out.

Dismissing the Dutch

On the way back to the station, I try to catch up with the twenty-five texts I have been sent from Cyril, Cheng, and my wife. Her latest says simply, "Where are you?" I have no choice but to drop by the hospital to check on Jimmy. Crashing through the quiet of the hospital, I race to his bed. 'What's wrong?' I ask drawing the attention of everyone in the ward.

'Nothing dear,' Bophra replies, 'I just needed to know where you were, he's still sleeping.'

I start to shout and curse, then I realise that she has been here since yesterday without relief. 'Why not call your mother?'

'But she told me to give him the...' she whimpers and turns away. She is afraid of my possible reaction.

'Well, just make sure you don't ever listen to her advice again. And you tell her that if he does not recover, she will be with her ancestors a darn sight sooner than she expected.'

Bophra looks shocked at me, and then nods. When we married, she was the most beautiful girl from her village. I had found her eager to learn and fantastic support, as she was a hundred percent dedicated to me and my career. Things had progressed well with Jenny; she was an astonishingly good mother. Then there was a gap; the son who was to have completed our family didn't materialise. When Jimmy did come along with his problems, Bophra retreated into her shell. No longer the up-and-coming middle-class mum, she was once again the frightened, backward village girl.

'You need your mother's support at the moment. Tell her to come down and take over with Jimmy, whilst you go and get some rest.' With that, I kiss Jimmy on the forehead. Turning to kiss Bophra, I am foiled as she turns her head away. I storm back out of the hospital ward, leaving flustered nurses in my wake. I am now ready for those bloody Dutch kids, then on to the French women.

'We are political prisoners,' Isabella Van Arle is shouting at me, whilst the Dutch Consulate official who has flown in from Phnom Penh this morning just sits and grimaces in his crumpled grey suit. It appears that she and the official are fluent in English, which is appealing, as I doubt whether we have easy access to any Dutch interpreters.

'I thought you were murderers?' I reply in a monotone. I don't want to inflame this young woman any more than I have to; she seems incendiary enough with her long bare arms flailing and her thin jaw jutting out like a claw hammer.

'The murderers are Leap Son and his like, and your government for allowing the trade in dog meat,' she answers, pointing at me with beautifully manicured nails.

'So, you retract your confession that you gave my officers yesterday?' I keep my face as bland as a *Star Trek* robot.

'Both of them do,' the official interjects.

'Who are you speaking for? Me?' She trains her bile on to the poor sweaty young man who had apologised for the "youth of the Nederlands" to me in very poor Cambodian when I met him in the office outside.

'Ms Van Arle. You have confessed to a capital crime. We don't kill murderers in Cambodia, nor do we treat them particularly well in prison,' a phrase I had used on the young American and I am sure will use again. 'If you did not kill Mr Son, and yet continue to profess your guilt and we find you could not have done so, then we will charge you with wasting police time, disrespect for the King of Cambodia's officials and public deceit. All of them carry prison sentences, large fines, and expulsion. I will leave you to ponder this. Your official must now accompany me to have the same conversation with Mr Van Buden.'

I deliver the same information to her partner in crime and then leave them both to fret whilst we chat in the lobby. The Dutch Consular official asks me, 'You won't prosecute, will you?'

'If you can get them to withdraw their confessions by lunchtime, I will make sure that they are on the next plane out of the country. They are of no use to me as witnesses and I don't believe a word they say. We will be sending a bill for police time to your embassy. You can decide who pays it.'

'I protest,' he replies, stamping his right foot.

'OK, they have thirty days in a cell for wasting our time and a fifty thousand US Dollar fine each,' I say with casual disregard for the poor official.

'You are not a judge here, Chief Inspector.' He is now trying to puff out his chest, which merely exaggerates his unkempt and dishevelled appearance. It takes years of acclimatisation to wear a full suit in the Cambodian heat without the crutch of air-con.

'I know but Cambodia is Cambodia. Check with your lords and masters, the price goes up tomorrow.' I leave the poor young official to plead with his errant subjects. Just time for a spot of lunch with my daughter before finally tackling the French and killing off this case. I decide the Ta Prohm murders can be left until tomorrow by which time all the forensics will be in, and the mountain of CCTV will have been scoured. Hopefully, the blood on the temple floors will have been cleared sufficiently for the tourist hordes not to notice. Knowing our crafty guides the stains will be included in some lurid tale of blood sacrifice.

I have told Cheng to leave each lady in a humid room for an hour before I arrive. The French Consulate official who I have met on several previous occasions is far more experienced than his Dutch counterpart and a fluent Cambodian speaker. I enjoy both his dry wit and intelligence.

'This is a bad business, Michael.' He has been down at the French Bakery off Wat Bo Road, and still has signs of their excellent croissant on his lightweight tailored suit.

Noticing my look he flicks off the crumbs in a casual Gallic way. 'That Charles, he bakes a mean pastry,' he says in perfect, if a bit posh, Cambodian.

'So, what am I to do, Henry?' I ask. 'They have both confessed to garrotting him. They were behind him on the bus and there was a broken shoelace which matches one of the lady's missing shoes! They are as guilty as Nixon!'

Henry laughs laconically. 'Let us see what they say in front of me, my friend. You never know.'

We start with Lavande, the younger and I think the weaker of the two.

Immediately as we enter the smelly, sweaty room Henry says, 'But my dear Chief Inspector, your air-conditioning seems to be on the blink.' He moves to the wall, fiddles with our control panel. 'Now that will be better.' A blast of cool air flows from the ceiling. Delacor has missed his vocation; I could never have managed that engineering feat.

'And your man has forgotten to bring in some fresh water! How remiss of you, Michael,' he motions to Cheng to get some water. 'Mademoiselle,' he bows gracefully to Lavande, 'I am your consular representative, Henry Delacor. Have you eaten well this morning?'

Lavande, who had been hunched over, looking pretty beaten, springs up under the charm of Henry, 'Oh no, Monsieur, the food is terrible!'

'Extraordinary! Cambodia is so full of good food, well luckily I have some extra pain au chocolat from breakfast and I am sure the inspector will get you an iced coffee, with sweet milk or black?'

'Black please, Monsieur, I can't stand that filthy American condensed milk.' My best-laid plans of intimidating her are scuppered by Henry.

'So, Mademoiselle, I understand there was a commotion on the Angkor Express,' Henry starts.

'And that Henry is enough,' I interrupt. 'Mademoiselle Hough,' if that is what Henry calls her, then so will I. 'Monsieur Delacor is your French Consulate representative, he is not your lawyer and has no right to speak, except in certain very defined areas. You may ask him for his advice, but I caution you again HE IS NOT A LAWYER.' I articulate this very clearly, as this is a very important point. 'He should not be treated as such.' Henry smiles and performs another shrug, as I put him back in his box. I know he is both fair and fastidious; I will have to run things by the book now.

'Before we get into the meat of anything, I have to explain, Mademoiselle, that you don't need to be cautioned. In Cambodia, we simply expect that you will always tell a representative of the King the truth. Any falsehoods spoken to any official are considered to be punishable offences. Do you understand this?'

'You are no better than the Khmer Rouge who went before you then,' she replies, jutting her head forward.

'I will also tell you that everything you say in this room, whether it is to me or Monsieur Delacor, is being recorded. Only when you have a lawyer, will you have any privacy. Now you are here because you have confessed to killing Mr Leap Son on the Angkor Express bus two days ago. Is this still your position?'

She is very quiet, which I feel is ominous. I don't need her to start quibbling at this point. I have another bloody murder to go and solve, rather than this bloodless one.

'I don't think I killed him,' she says.

'What?' I am shocked. I hadn't expected this.

'I think he was already dead when I strangled him.' She shrivels up like a hedgehog into a ball in front of me. 'And Jasmine couldn't have done it anyway, her wrists are crippled with arthritis.' She mimics shrivelled hands, something I had failed to notice in her sister. 'I did, however, put the shoelace around his neck and pull it so hard that it broke. He didn't struggle at all. He should have struggled even if drunk or asleep. Jasmine and I argued. She said we must have killed him, but I don't think we did. Can you tell? I can't live with myself actually killing someone, it is too dreadful. Even if he was a vicious, murdering bastard.'

Shit. I leave the room, with Henry in my wake, abandoning the now weeping Lavande. I text Dr Pang, "Could Son have been dead when he was strangled?"

Henry burst out laughing, 'So, what if Nixon had only been guilty in thought and not actually in deed? And didn't he get away with it in the end?'

I recompose myself. 'I will get back to you, Henry. Go and have another coffee and I will send a man when we have more news.'

Could he have been dead before he was stabbed and before he was strangled? Who killed Son?

The Autopsy

Cyril and I stood looking through the glass window into the autopsy room. We communicate with the doctor through the intercom, although his voice is muffled by the face mask and nose plugs. Autopsies in Cambodia are never the clean-looking affairs of the movies. Here there is blood and guts scattered across the stainless steel workbenches and the smell is appalling.

'So, what killed him, doctor?' asks Cyril, who has joined me after I told him of my debacle with Lavande and Henry.

'This is not an exact science, gentlemen, and I am not equipped to manage such complicated affairs,' he mumbles.

'Do I need to bring in an expert?' Cyril quips cheerfully.

The reply sounds like "fuck off". The doctor is a good Buddhist and would never say that. Cyril and I laugh.

'Maybe we have no one cause. The dagger didn't kill him, there was no blood. He was certainly dead when he was stabbed.'

'So not the American,' I confirm.

'Now we have the shoelace. Unfortunately, this could never have killed him, just not strong enough, and anyway, he was already dead when it was applied.'

'So not the French sisters,' My list of suspects is diminishing.

'Now I have the puncture wound I had mentioned in his shoulder. It is consistent with a needle.'

'Was he dead when it was inserted?' I ask.

'That is a tricky one, "possibly" would be my answer. There is some bruising which you only get when blood is circulating but…'

'Thank you, doctor,' says Cyril, holding me back, 'we appreciate the difficulties. We do need an answer both to the cause of death and what was in that syringe. Have you any ideas on that?'

Sonith turns to look at us through the glass, he seems to have some intestines in his hand, like a trader in the meat market. 'The answer will be here or not,' he says cryptically.

'Which means?' I ask.

'If I find toxicity here, then he has been killed by the syringe; if not, then I will check the tissue in that area. Both require more time and better equipment. For now, just find out who injected him and then later we can see if they killed him.'

'Do we know what was injected?' asks Cyril.

'Well, his clothes and shoulder are covered in high-grade heroin, which I would think is a big clue, but I can't be sure until I have one hundred percent tested both areas.'

'Heroin?' Both Cyril and I say at the same time.

'Yes, very pure, very high quality, too good for common smugglers,' the doctor adds.

As Bophra was now home, I send Jenny out of the station, this case is getting grizzly. Luckily, she hasn't seen the files on the two tortured Cambodians. Cheng has made sure of that. So, Cyril and I are sitting in his office having an iced coffee. We luxuriate in the sweetness from the condensed milk; there is no need for extra sugar.

'What is your next move, Michael?' Cyril asks in his gentle way.

'I'm running out of suspects. I released the sisters to a laughing Henry, but I still have the French couple, the young Vietnamese, the older English couple, and the Romanians left. I honestly thought they were all just innocent bystanders. The initial interviews show nothing but tourist activities. I suppose I will have to try again. I have comprehensive files on their movements from Sergeant Munny, he seems to be trying extra hard to make up for his disloyalty.'

'To worm his way back in?'

'The Romanians are due to fly home tomorrow, so I guess I will start with them; at least they don't have consular support, which is pretty telling. Cheng has them waiting for me. I will do the rest in their hotels this evening and report to you in the morning. I don't want to keep them from flying out, but if I need to, can I?'

'I think we may have to. I'll sort out the niceties with the embassies involved. No doubt the Vietnamese will complain the loudest, at least all the Europeans will be covered by insurance.'

'Thank you, sir. Do you think it odd that we haven't heard from General Cho? He was all over us at the start of this, what do you think his involvement is?' I am concerned after the threats he made.

'Probably the least said the better,' Cyril says. 'The general is tied up with the Sam Rainsy threat and so has hopefully moved on from this.'

The ex-opposition leader is still in the news despite stories that he was stopped from leaving France. The threat of revolution hangs around like a bad leak of sewage. No one tells us mere police what is going on, we are not in the security systems' "What's Ap" group.

'Yes, but why was he so concerned with Son at the start?'

Cyril simply puts a finger to his lips. 'I've been on the phone Michael. Remember, we all work for the King, now go finish this investigation. Ta Prohm temple is being reopened in the morning, and there will not be a press release.'

I can't say I am shocked by Cyril's position. He is telling me that there is something deeper here. Is Son involved with the exiled opposition leader and his threats to return and undermine the King? I guess that he could be some type of fixer for the opposition? So, he could have been killed by a secret service operator on the bus? Possibly this may have been the couple slaughtered in the temple? If so, who murdered them and why? Will I ever find out?

Reading the file of the Stoica's showed them to be an odd couple of visitors. We saw a rush of Russian tourists about ten years ago, which has now diminished to a trickle as the rouble has fallen. Eastern Europeans are normally very young student types, the first generation of travellers. The older ones normally go to cheaper destinations. The Stoicas had flown in via Bangkok to Siem Reap, then taken the bus to Battambang, staying at the Stung Sangke hotel for two days. My report from Munny said they stayed inside the entire time, not taking any trips. The hotel has a pool, but they didn't seem to frequent it at all. Then they returned on the same six-hour bus and are now due to go home tomorrow, without visiting Angkor Wat.

Entering the interview room with Florin Stoica, my cop senses go flying through the roof; this one is bad. He is well-muscled, mid-thirties with a heavy-set face. I can't see much through his long sleeve shirt, however, poking from under the cuffs are signs of heavy tattoos. I understand that this is all the rage amongst Western youngsters and gangsters. He smacks of the latter.

'How have you enjoyed your time in Cambodia Mr Stoica?' I ask in my monotone voice.

'It has been agreeable.' He speaks very coherently with a heavily accented tongue, conflicting with my notes, which say he is very poor at English.

'Did you enjoy Battambang, the bamboo railway or the ancient temples?'

'We were unwell and stayed in the hotel.'

This, however, is word perfect from his previous statement. 'And the temples of Angkor Wat?'

'The trouble on the bus upset my wife,' he replies in a monotone matching mine, as if he is trying to keep his replies uninteresting.

'So, you have come some eight thousand kilometres and not seen or done anything except take two pretty uncomfortable bus trips?' Even I can't hide my incredulity.

'We have done nothing wrong. Why have you said we would have to miss our flight tomorrow?'

Is he starting to get rattled? I can imagine he would be a real threat if you met him in a dark alley somewhere. I know he has done something wrong, but what? We have been through Son's telephone records and found many one-off use numbers, a couple of which we could trace to a phone card sold at a store based at Siem Reap airport arrivals. Munny checked, but neither Florin nor his wife admit that they had bought a SIM card. People who don't want their phone calls traced often persuade the shops not to record the names of their clients as accurately as they should.

Working on my intuition, I take two and two and make four. 'I understand your frustration, but we need to clear up your phone SIM card situation.'

'I don't have a Cambodian sim,' he retorts sharply.

'We showed your picture to the phone card traders.' He twitches as I say this. That inner chimp of his is starting to rattle hard on its cage. 'One of them identified you as the purchaser of a SIM card.' This is an outlandish lie. I might have to delete this bit from the recorded interview later.

'Ha!' he smiles. 'I did not buy a SIM card.'

Realising my mistake, I correct myself, 'Sorry my English was not perfect there. I meant "your wife", grammar is different in Cambodian. The trader will testify to the fact that he sold her a Cambodian SIM card on your arrival. We have the number and the fact that it has been used to contact the murder victim's phone.' The trader would stand up in court and say he sold a phone card to ET and Elvis if I told him to.

This time I watch as Florin's hands flinch, his shoulders tighten, and his pupils dilate. I have no idea what this all means, or what he has done, but it is interesting stuff.

'I am asking you some simple questions and will not let you leave here until I have the answers. Why did you come all the way to Cambodia and not visit anywhere? Why did you take the Angkor Express twice? And why did you ring the dead man Leap Son the night before boarding the bus?'

He sits there, looks deeply into my eyes. 'Fuck you, you don't know who you are dealing with.'

'We shall see, Mr Stoica. I think you can stay here until you have an answer for me. We will, of course, have to check you out for drugs.' With that, I leave him stewing. I know that the comprehensive searches Cheng will put him through will ensure that Florin will have to refrain from sitting for the rest of the day.

The English Connection

I manage to meet Jenny and her school friends at a food stall outside the night market and buy them all fritters. It is my only supper. The double-fried bananas are not only delicious but also very filling. The vendor is opposite the Ta Prohm Hotel which must be doing a special for independent tourists as the English couple, the Jones's are also staying here.

I have given up on Sofia Stoica as she either speaks no English or is a remarkable actor. We don't have a broad range of language experts in Siem Reap, and certainly not a Romanian speaker. We have been forced previously to give up using Google translate as even our judges felt this was inappropriate. I asked for an online interpreter, but Cyril declined my request on cost grounds. Instead, I have arranged similar body searches for Mrs Stoica. All I know is that the Romanians are bad and that they have been in contact with Son. They do not appear to have a motive to kill him.

Who the hell was Leap Son, though? He seems to have more tentacles than a squid, and each deep in a murky trade. Then there is the general, but I have found nothing to connect the two. Is Son just a major criminal we had never heard of? Could he be the murdering colonel of the hospital back in the bad old days? Is this all Khmer Rouge business alive and well in twenty-first-century Cambodia?

The file on the English is very bland. They seem to fit exactly the tourist profile, even if it is Mrs Jones who has done all the excursions, whilst Mr Jones has been spending his time merely wandering around the town. I will ask about that. They are on newish passports and have come in via Thailand overland, which is pretty eccentric for such an old couple, who are in their late fifties with neither looking overly fit.

Back in the Ta Prohm hotel temporary interview room, I give them a joint interview to save time.

'Mr and Ms Jones, thank you for your time,' I start with a smile. Mr Jones returns this and leans back in his chair, exuding that confidence of a man used to being in charge. He appears content with the current situation. Mrs Jones is far more excitable. Maybe I should have seen them on their own?

'Have you found out what happened to that poor man?' she asks me first. 'I can't believe those Dutch youngsters did anything, and where could they find a knife? I couldn't find one to cut the mango I bought.' It seems she talks in a stream of consciousness, which Mr Jones ignores as he watches me.

'No, it wasn't the Dutch couple. They seem to have used this as a publicity stunt,' I reply, desperately trying to retake control.

'Oh, dog meat, isn't that awful? I didn't know it was legal here, and who would eat some of those animals anyway?' she continues unabated.

Mr Jones leans forward, physically cutting across his wife. 'I'm sure we are supposed to answer the questions and not ask them, dear. Pardon but I don't know your rank?' His manner was that of a superior officer, a man well used to asking the questions.

'I am sorry, I am Chief Inspector Suon.'

'The same name as the chap who died?' he asks.

'No, he was Leap Son.'

He hums, seeming to be confused by my answer. 'Well, Chief Inspector, how can we help you? We were way behind him on the bus,' he continues in his confident manner.

Ignoring his questions, I ask, 'You don't appear to be a very good tourist, Mr Jones. Your lady wife was on her own touring the bamboo railway and the Ek Phnom temple in Battambang. And I understand you avoided our boat trip?' Maybe this would shake him.

'Yes, she likes to do all the tours. I prefer just to soak up the atmosphere, sit by the pool and drink the beer. I'm sure your chaps who are asking around will tell you that. You didn't know that we took the boat down from here to Battambang? It was a bit noisy for me and the levels of plastic waste in the river rather put me off. You need to do something about that, Inspector.'

He's playing with me. 'Chief Inspector,' I reply a bit testily.

'So, I'm not a great tourist. What else do you want to know? We are planning on a last night meal before we fly to Hanoi tomorrow.' He looks at his watch.

'Darling, we can always delay the flight,' she interjects.

A quick flash of annoyance passes across his face, 'Not without a penalty, darling. It's the 8.30 flight tomorrow night.' He is not a man to be crossed, but who is he?

'Is it your annual holiday, Mrs Jones?' It was her turn to look flustered, but she recovers well.

'No, we are retired. We travel most of the year, and we have a month in Vietnam after this.'

'You don't work then?' I press as they seem far too young to be retired.

'Goodness no!' they laugh together. I am not sure whether this is genuine, although I have heard that life is easier in Europe. I didn't think you could retire in your mid-fifties.

'We are the gratefully unemployed,' he says with glee.

'Where were you yesterday?' I am scraping the barrel for questions now.

'We went to the temples with Loren and Denise, we all shared a car. It was our third day of the Angkor Wat complex, so we did the outer temples,' Mrs Jones replies. 'But we got separated just as we saw the couple from the back of the bus; you know the well-dressed ones.'

'What?' I splutter, surprised that I have struck gold.

'Yes, we saw the couple who had left the bus on the outskirts of town. When we saw the pair at Angkor Wat, Loren suddenly said that they had to fly and could we get another lift back. He said he would pay for the car.'

'It was a bit bloody inconvenient really, but it saved us a packet as we got a Grab taxi back for only five dollars,' Mr Jones interjected. He was smiling again. 'Does that help you, Chief Inspector?' His look is almost gleeful.

Does he know something? We haven't released the details of the deaths to the public. We are a secretive bunch and like to catch the perpetrators before we ever tell the press. With the general involved, this case may never be made public.

With a sudden flash of intuition I realise, Mr Jones was "police". 'Yes, that is very helpful. Have you seen your French friends since?'

'Well now you ask, we haven't. They were not in the hotel bar last night or at breakfast, and we were hoping to get them on Facebook.' Mr Jones is the epitome of innocence, reaching out and holding his wife's hand.

Is he giving me a lead or is the investigation getting to me? 'And the other bus guests?' I ask.

'Oh no, I don't think any of the others would be good Facebook contacts.' Mrs Jones was emphatic. 'The Romanians are a rum couple, if you ask me. I can't put my finger on it, but they seem a bit odd.'

'That Vietnamese couple were so out of place. They seemed more fascinated about the UK than Angkor Wat. They said that their ambition was to go to England,' he adds.

Mrs Jones continues, 'They were very excited at the start of the trip. They told me they had found a way to get into England but were still not sure. I asked them about the recent immigrants who had died in the frozen container and they both looked very upset. I don't think that they had heard the news. They told me that they had spent two weeks in Battambang on honeymoon. Having been there, it seems a strange place to have a special holiday. It's a bit of a dump.'

'You two seem to be doing my job for me.' I am smiling now, wishing I had talked to these two earlier on in my investigation.

'We are always pleased to help,' he replies, 'and the Romanian, do you have him?'

So, they were not tourists and not murderers themselves, but they knew all about the crimes that were being committed on the bus. Hmm, Cyril would love this.

'Well thank you both,' I call the interview to a halt. 'I'm sure you will have no problems with your flight tomorrow.

Could I ask that you both stay unemployed whilst you are in Cambodia?'

Everything is clear to me now.

Conclusion

Picking up Kiry and Pich Nimol takes no time, and they soon confess to wanting to be smuggled to England. They had been given Leap Son as a contact and were being passed over to Florin Stoica, who was supervising the first collection of a group to go over the border. This cleared the Romanians as murderers. Cyril will talk to Interpol and pass all their details on, although I somehow know that Mr Jones already has this well in hand.

Samnang, my colleague in the tourist police and drugs unit, is extremely pleased with the information about our young American. I will be able to use this as a quid pro quo when the moment is right. A bank of favours is worth more than gold.

The report I send to General Cho says that Leap Son died of natural causes. There is no report on the deaths at Ta Prohm temple, so I am not looking for the French couple, Loren and Denise. The general came back to Cyril and said he was full of praise for my investigations. He told him that I had done a marvellous job for the king and that we would all be rewarded.

Cheng is now reassigned as my new corporal and Munny will be given a staff sergeant role with one of the general's groups in the north of the province, far away from us.

Cyril has set about cleaning up all of Son's operations, and for good measure, will be closing down the dog meat factory so we can look forward to a good reaction from the international press.

I feel this is one back for Jimmy who seems to be recovering well as he sits and plays with toy cars in the corner of the office whilst Doctor Pang, Cyril and I indulge in a fantastic snake wine the English couple had delivered to the station with a card which had just said "Thanks".

Doctor Pang explains that in the end Leap Son died of a heart attack soon after he had sat on the bus, his arteries as clogged as the streets of Phnom Penh. We presume that the heroin jab was delivered by the young Cambodians, who we believe were agents working for the general. Evidently, Leap Son had taken one risk too many. Linking him to counter-revolution would be an unwise course for us to even contemplate.

'It just goes to show a bad diet is more dangerous than heroin, a garrote and a knife,' laughs the doctor uncharacteristically jovially.

'So, it was not "Murder" on the "Angkor Express" then,' laughs Cyril, 'just natural causes. Who will believe us when we say that?'

'The truly horrible murder will be covered up.' Following a quiet word with Henry Delacor, he had told me that the French government were not interested in Loren and Denise and would take no action unless someone asked about them, which he expected would never happen. They are a remnant of past times, events we would all rather forget.

'I take it we have freed the French ladies and the Dutch kids then?' asks the doctor.

'With a healthy financial contribution from France and Holland, this investigation has been good for our coffers, even after your expensive lab tests, Doctor. So cheers to our much-hated colonial oppressors.' We drink to Cyril's toast.

'And who are the Jones's then, Michael?'

'I think the British still think that they are the world's police. I'm sure he is a senior officer sent to follow up people traffickers over here. They leave on the eight-thirty pm flight to Hanoi.'

'I didn't know that tourist buses were so interesting,' says the doctor. 'Now you pass me some more of that great snake wine Chief Inspector. Then we can catch the last of the Dragon boat races, I understand the forensics team are in the final against the firefighters!'

Fin

The Perfect Murder

Looking out from the twentieth floor window of the Peninsula Hotel in Singapore, the city-state spreads beneath me. In essence, it is a living replica of my hometown, Siem Reap, with the buildings draped in vibrant jungle clothing. I was here to attend a global policing conference on cold cases, specifically a series of workshops intended to "increase cross border synchronisation with old and unsolved murders". This was my reward for keeping a certain Chinese government employee's child from hitting the global headlines. I would have preferred a pay rise or a bonus, something I could have spent on my kids to make up for the time I had wasted at work.

All the delegates had met for pre-conference drinks, and I had been intrigued by my co-teammates. Each of us had been asked to submit a crime many weeks ago, to allow the organisers to build teams who could complement each other. I am sure they dreamed of us cracking a major case and so justifying the ridiculous costs of the whole affair. Cyril, my boss, had told me not to worry about anything apart from the minibar. If I touched that, my future career was in dire peril. I had deliberately moved a heavy bedroom chair in front of my Pandora's box.

'So, I can charge drinks to my room then?' I had asked.

'No,' he had replied, and we had left it at that. I had been given one hundred dollars for expenses; the hotel was full board, and I was required to keep receipts for everything I spent. All I intended to spend outside the hotel was perfume for my wife and daughter and some Lego for my son. For the rest I would be abstemious, I had no desire to run up a large drinks bills.

The conference kicked off with a session from each of the major sponsors. The FBI had bored us with their latest stupidly expensive CSI technology, the Brits had talked pompously about intelligence-led policing and the Chinese had shown the latest facial recognition software which they had combined with the track and trace COVID Apps and now extended into post-pandemic Chinese life. Big Brother is alive and kicking in Beijing.

My first surprise had been that the regional coordinator who introduced our group together was a familiar face.

'Hi, I'm Commander Bob Jones from the UK City of London Police (Retired), and I am coordinating the Far East regional groups,' he said. He was dressed in a very smart civilian grey suit and a strange bright orange and gold striped silk tie. He was still large as I remembered him from our previous meeting, but the suit and tie seemed to melt him into the correct proportions, ending with the impression of being impressive rather than fat.

Bob briefly introduced all the team to each other: David Chin from Hong Kong, Lei Fat from Chengdu, Richie Robinson from Washington, and Nisha Singh from Mumbai. He told us that our last member was on his way and would be with us in the morning. Then that we would have a formal team get-to-know first thing after breakfast.

As he made to move off, I Intercepted him saying, 'Mr Jones, what a surprise.'

I would have expected him to have shown at least a trace of embarrassment, as the last time we had met he had been working undercover, specifically without my government's permission, in Cambodia. But not a jot. He simply smiled and said, 'Chief Inspector Suon, I am so pleased that your government released you for this. I'm looking forward to working with you in a less covert way. Now I have to get on, plenty of teams to coalesce.' And with that, he melted into the crowd.

For the rest of the evening, I took full advantage of the free food and drinks on offer. At ten o'clock, these ceased and there was a general movement towards the bar. I left, came back to the room and, with a local Sim I had bought at the airport, rang home. Nine o'clock is pushing it, but the whole family was up waiting to hear from me. I showed them the night view from my room, the massive queen- sized bed and the luxurious marble bathroom. Redolent with love and kisses, I fell asleep dreaming of luxury and smoked salmon canapes.

We had been told that we were going to be team building, which involved external trainers. I had heard of executive coaching and team development from passing references on Western TV programmes and was nervous, to say the least. Cyril and General Cho had given me strict instructions that I was not to disgrace the force, embarrass Cambodia or in any way give out any information that they had not previously sanctioned. We had sweated over which "cold case" to declare for the course, and at one point we had decided that as we don't ever admit to not solving a case, that the whole process was pointless. Eventually, however, it had been suggested that we use the case of murdered Australian tourist Evelyn Vaughn.

Calling it a cold case was rather stretching the truth as we had technically closed it by way of a "suicide by cop" shoot-out. The main suspect, Che Lo, was killed by our internal security forces, who had been hunting him for months. Dead suspects don't generally get much say in the process of defining guilt, so he was posthumously found guilty of a number of murders, many of which had nothing to do with him.

Evelyn had been killed at the Ballang temple, some forty kilometres from Angkor Wat proper at the edge of the Phnom Kulen National Park. Some tourists barely manage to cover the main temple site; she must have been a real enthusiast.

The body was found alone with her E-bike. Her head was lying by her side. She had been decapitated by a mighty slash from a seriously large blade. Doctor Pang, our pathologist, had compiled a file and sent it to central records in Phnom Penh. We were told to close the case soon after and assign the murder to Che Lo. At the time I had asked for some resources to investigate further as I had an eyewitness who reported a dark car driving past the Kneeling Elephant statue five hundred metres from the murder site. I was told not to bother, so I didn't. There are times not to push. Why would I want to take on the case of a murdered tourist where the culprit was almost certainly dead? There are no prizes in Cambodia for finding your superiors have fucked up, especially when internal security is involved.

In the morning, with a most comprehensive breakfast stashed away, I joined my fellow colleagues for our team-building session. You have to admire the poor facilitators who tried to winkle out cooperation from us. They did at least manage to get everybody to introduce themselves.

Richie Robinson was our FBI forensics expert, based in Washington DC on the east coast of the USA, although, as he said many times, he is really a surf boy from California. With his easy smile and expensive suit, he looked as if he was straight from NCIS and I was immediately concerned about my lack of worldliness. Manfully, he supported Suzie, the facilitator, in trying to uncover our personality traits. Evidently, this introspective personal stuff is common in the USA.

This was all too much for Lei Fat the chubby sallow young man from Chengdu. He had to leave after being questioned on his first pet's name, unfortunately, this was too similar to a technique used by Chinese special investigators on suspected traitors. Lei returned later with a Chinese official and Commander Jones and was excused the rest of the exercise. We did find out that his specialism was mass surveillance having managed a project to install cameras in Chengdu airport.

David Chin, the spotty and somewhat nerdy Chinese Hong Kong security agent, was an expert in audio files. His speciality was in filtering out background sounds from security taps to uncover what suspects were mumbling during undercover ops. We learnt that there is no point in turning taps on in a room to enable you to avoid a "bug" a la James Bond. He said he could eliminate the background noise generated by

Niagara Falls even if you were sitting in the *Maid of the Mist* boat getting sprayed with water. He was somewhat scary and even Lei Fat looked impressed.

Nisha Singh took the whole exercise in her stride. As the only Indian, only woman, and only non-law enforcement officer, she seemed rather out of place. Nisha is a securities lawyer who has been working with Interpol to track and trace the money from many international frauds. I asked her why she was here and were there many cold cases in India?

She said dismissively, 'Unless the police catch the culprit red-handed, there are only cold cases in India. especially if you are a woman who has been attacked by a man.' She looked at me with her dark brown eyes, past her chiselled aquiline nose and down through my soul. I wished to apologise for policemen everywhere. Then she completely changed and added airily, 'So, I'm here to help you guys put a stop to that.' Her pearlescent white teeth flashed a Bollywood smile at us all leaving us enthralled like the dwarfs around Cinderella.

I was, in fact, the most senior officer in the group with our final member, Doug Houet from Oz being little more than a state trooper. He was on the Darwin police force and seemed to spend a not inconsiderable amount of his life wandering around the outback of Northern Australia looking for the remains of lost tourists. I couldn't help but think of him as Crocodile Dundee, without the flashing good looks of Paul Hogan.

Suzie, our British HR consultant who had cajoled us through her team-building exercises, took her bows and expressed a fervent desire for a Singapore Sling. 'Team,' she said, 'I wish you good luck. I may see you tonight after I have spent this afternoon relaxing at Sentosa.'

I found out that Singapore has an island dedicated to pleasure. What a place!

'Well, chaps are we now all together?' Our leader, Commander Jones (retired) came in at about eleven. 'Now I want you all to read each other's crime files for the next hour and choose which one you will jointly investigate. I have my favourite, but I'm letting you decide.' And off he went again.

'So, who is in charge?' asked Lei.

We all looked towards the floor. This was not a time to be jumping to the front of the queue. Another choice phrase from Cyril came to my mind, "Don't fucking show off, Michael".

Nisha laughed, 'Well, you are a lot of pushy Alpha males. I would have thought that this would be an opportunity for you to show off!'

Doug, the Oz sucked in some air. 'Look, this is the police and I guess Michael here is the most senior officer, so I'm willing to let him lead, as long as we all have our say.'

I turned and looked at Doug, aghast.

'Yep, I agree,' said Richie. 'I was told that we should follow standard protocol, and a Chief Inspector ranks me easily. It's your game, Michael.'

Lei Fat was very pleased as he smiled and nodded. 'I think we should follow Chief Inspector Suon and take his case.'

'Hold on there, Lei, I haven't read the cases yet,' said Nisha. 'How come you have?'

Lei looked a bit shaken. 'I asked for extra reading time, as they are only in English, sorry.' He hung his head in shame, thus diffusing any international tension.

I made up my mind. 'OK, I will take the lead on the investigation, but only very loosely. This is supposed to be a collaborative effort. As far as whose project we use, I suggest that we read for an hour and then each proposes their favourite. If there is a clear winner, let's do that. If not, then we can vote.' It was a rather longer speech than I had intended.

'Excellent,' said David, taking a sheaf of papers, filling up his coffee, and going to the corner.

How I wished now I could call for a Cambodian coffee with sweet milk. I needed that spurt of energy. Apart from the Commander popping his head around our door and giving the thumbs up, we all worked without interruption for the next hour.

'Ok, then,' I said eventually. 'Any objections to just going around the room? Lei, have you changed your mind?'

Lei looked up and put up both thumbs. 'I like your "Murder in the Temple" case. It's international, loads of CCTV and I'm sure my data mining could help.'

Doug was next. 'Yeh, well I was hoping for a bit of help with my missing Romanian. We only found his boots in the stomach of an old croc, but I like your case too as it has a north Australian link.'

Nisha pulled back her long black hair and said, 'Your case, Michael. If I'm not too mistaken there could be a need for some forensic accounting and a deep dive into business ownership.'

'Well, as long as you all agree, I want it too. I see that there is a phone call about the time of the murder, maybe I could analyse the audio files?' said David.

It was looking like I had no way out.

'Sorry to disappoint Michael.' Richie was showing an acute understanding of my facial expression. 'I would love to get my hands on the files re your blade; that sounds like a weird murder stroke.'

'Well,' I laughed, 'my boss will be pleased.'

Commander Jones chose that moment to burst into the room. 'People, have we got a case?'

'Yes, Commander,' I said.

'Call me Bob here, Michael. Which one?'

'Unanimous. "Murder at Ballang Temple",' said Nisha dramatically.

'More like "The Perfect Murder",' said Richie.

'Great, off to lunch, then back to the theatre. One of our chaps has an interesting take on the Jack the Ripper murders,' Bob said, leaving our escape hatch open for the first time that morning.

When we got back after lunch, all the walls had been covered in a continuous roll of white paper.

'Someone has been busy,' said Nisha.

Richie smiled and said, 'I find it a cool way to share all the data. I never have enough room on the incident boards they give me.'

I thought back to the chalkboards in our "incident room", or my office as we normally called it, and smiled.

'So how are we going to approach this Chief Inspector?' asked Lei formally.

Lei showed a love of structure and order, what I would expect from juniors, whereas Richie, Doug, and Nisha all seemed quite happy to act independently. Herding these cats could be a problem I have never had to deal with before.

'Well, for a start, I propose we drop any titles. Then let's use this wallcovering to plot the murder. I don't think we need to work separately yet. Let's all understand the timeline and, as it was my crime, I guess this is my job.'

I laid out the case as we had known it and the evidence that we had gathered before being told to call a halt. The victim Evelyn Vaughn had been in Cambodia for three weeks, travelling across the country, visiting not only the main tourist sites but also the more obscure temples. Occasionally she had joined tour groups. Other tourists who had met her said that she was often better informed than the guides. She appeared to have a deep understanding of the Hindu faith and the Hindu history of Cambodia. Interestingly, she paid scant regard to the Buddhist sites or anything to do with our more recent bloody history.

Evelyn was single-minded about her endeavours. We had found copious notes and papers in her room at the Ta Prohm Hotel in town, and on her computer. There looked to be the start of either a story or a history based in Cambodia.

The temple, where her body was found, is covered by the general Angkor Wat pass ticket, but is neither patrolled nor covered by CCTV. It is at the dead-end of a dirt road and only has a fortnightly clear up crew visit and all they do is check for rubbish and graffiti every other Tuesday. The Kneeling Elephant carving some five hundred metres back towards the road is similarly rarely visited. A further kilometre past this to the local road junction where there is the tiny village of Khnang Phnum. A hardy native had been in the jungle on the Wednesday morning and says he saw a large dark car drive by.

My forensic pathologist, Doctor Pang, discerned the murder could have been committed between six to ten days before the body was found. As she was last seen on that Wednesday morning, at the hotel, and her body found the following Tuesday, this seemed to stack up. The decapitation was consistent with a large blade, like the Khmer Condor knife, which is thirty centimetres of wickedly sharp steel. It is a standard tool used by many villages. This same weapon had been used in a number of murders of single women over the previous few months. There had been no more incidents like this after the death of Che Lo two weeks after Evelyn's murder, a contributing reason why the case was considered solved.

We had checked out with the Australian Consulate any information that they had about Evelyn. Initially, there had been some confusion over her passport, as her name was Evelyn Amarak, not Vaughn. It had taken a few days for them to confirm that this was one and the same person. Evidently, Evelyn had married earlier in the year, and although her credit cards were in the name of Vaughn, she had not managed to change her passport in time for her trip. This, of course, also delayed us in contacting her family. The murder was kept out of the press until we had finally managed to get through to anyone who knew her in her hometown of Nauiyu in the Northern Territory of Australia. Her husband was not available, and it later turned out had apparently committed suicide burning himself in a car. Her ex-sister-in-law, Charlotte Vaughn, said she had not heard from Evelyn, as she had been on a retreat and had only returned on the previous Sunday.

Evelyn's phone records were sketchy, as she had switched her Australian SIM for a local one. We assumed that she was using data and some internet phone service, but have never been able to access anything from her accounts. The Australian police said that the husband didn't have a social media presence and that his phone was a "non" smart one. They did find a single message from Evelyn on his work answerphone.

I played the transcript from my phone. I don't know why, but I always have it on me; something about it bothers me.

"Darling, I really wish you were here. I have found this wonderful temple, which I think backs up my theory of the Hindu progression through the Mekong delta. It's all abandoned. They do that with anything which is not Buddhist here, cultural monogamists! I thought I would burn my International credit to wish you a happy birthday. I hope you are not working too hard and I will be home next week... Hello, is someone there? agh... aghhhhh..."

We didn't find her phone and presumed the murderer took it and disposed of it. There may well have been footprints and tyre tracks, but by the time our CSI team were on the scene, the area had been trampled by villagers, police, and countless vehicles.

I got one break when I found from Immigration that Evelyn's husband had, in fact, come out to Cambodia. I have a record from the Vietnam border by Ha Tien of entry by William Vaughn on Saturday prior to the murder and a cross border crossing to Thailand at Krong Poi Pet on the following Thursday. A day after, we assumed the murder was committed. Later we found out that the body of William was found in a burnt-out car on the following Friday, three days after we had found the body of Evelyn. However, they thought the car was probably burnt out on the Wednesday a couple of days earlier.

Looking up, I could see that the paper around the room was filling up with the details of the case. I had never had such a luxury as this. I found it made my blood rush.

'So, questions?' I asked.

Doug said, 'Look, guys I'm confused, this fell in my patch and I can hardly remember it, especially the link to her husband. Why wasn't it national news?'

I looked around the room, from the genuine confusion of Richie, David, and Lei, to the knowing look on Nisha's face.

'Come on Nisha, you seem to know something I don't. Why was this ignored in Australia?' Doug asked aggressively. Nisha looked at him straight in the eye. 'Because she was an Aborigine. This is all about racism, if she had been a white, blue-eyed, blonde bombshell, she would have been news, but a small, shy, black girl from arsewipe Northern Territory is hardly going to entice sympathy in the great unwashed of Australia.'

'Now, Nisha…' I interjected as we all looked at Doug.

'Ah,' was all he said. Was that an implicit agreement with Nisha's dismemberment of the Australian multicultural artifice, or just a deep knowledge of a certain element? I never asked Doug, I guess all societies have their dark soul, and this was theirs.

'So, the husband did it! Case closed,' said Lei, 'it is normally the husband.'

'But why travel through half of Asia to kill your new wife in a jungle just to come home, wait a week then kill yourself? No, I don't go for that,' said Richie. 'Look, if this part of

Australia is really the racist wild west that Nisha makes out, there must be tons of easier places to kill your wife. And do we know it is suicide? Who burns themselves in a car? Unless you are a modern-day Viking who wants to go to Valhalla in their chariot? It is a really painful way to go. Also, no note, nothing. It is extraordinary.'

David said, 'We may have trouble here if we use too many cultural references, like Vikings and Valhalla.'

'Oops,' said Richie, 'that's a good lesson for me. I'm far too "West Coast" American. Keep pulling me up, David.'

Doug said, 'Look guys, if a man has just killed his wife, he could be feeling remorse?'

'Doug, are you trying to whitewash this again? I can't believe anyone would switch so quickly from cunning murderer to remorseful husband!' Nisha said with finality.

David tried again. 'So, we agree that the husband is not the most likely murderer?' We all nodded. 'And therefore the "suicide" is now looking suspicious, then don't we have two murders?'

'But still only one murderer?' said Lei. 'That I am afraid would exclude your man who conveniently died in a hail of bullets, Michael.'

'It also throws the whole thing towards Australia and away from Cambodia. Well done Michael, you may be able to offshore this one!' said David.

'You are looking thoughtful, Nisha,' I said. I was still perplexed as to the value of a lawyer in a murder case, especially a non-criminal lawyer.

'I'm with Lei in the fact that the husband did it, but... if he didn't do it, surely the second law of policing is to follow the money?'

'What money?' I said. 'There was no great insurance cover for anyone to inherit, and no one has told me that there was great wealth here.'

'Well, you boys get on with your stuff. If I could borrow Doug, maybe we can find out if there is some grubby reason for murder most foul. I was told by my father's business partner in England, "Where there's muck there's brass".'

'Good idea,' I said, 'maybe we can use everyone's specialities.'

'I could look at the audio file on your phone. There might be more we can glean,' said David. 'Maybe Richie could get me access to some of that whizzy forensic machinery which the FBI has brought over?'

'Great idea, David,' I said, 'that leaves me and Lei to look at these movements by William Vaughn. If he wasn't here to kill his wife, why was he in Cambodia? And why such a convoluted itinerary? Do you think we can find some security footage of him somewhere, Lei? I have full access to our systems from here.'

Lei smiled, showing a set of yellowed teeth. 'I can find you a fart in a room of flatulent fat men.'

'Right, let's set a time for getting back together and report. Is five pm OK?'

There was a buzz of excitement as we all set off to deal with our special tasks. Could we possibly solve these cold murders in a hotel room in Singapore?

At five, we reconvened, with Commander Jones joining us.

'So, what did you think of the "Jack the Ripper" talk?' he asked.

Richie said, 'Surely we have seen it all before. The Canonical five were the only linked murders, the rest were copycats or attributed by a lazy press.'

'Yes, it is likely that the Ripper didn't kill all those victims,' Bob agreed, 'and how does that impact our case?'

'Well, our conclusion was predicated on there being a serial killer. So, we didn't follow up on an Australian connection after Che Lo was killed,' I said.

'And now what do you think?' Bob asked.

'I think we did a shit job,' Doug banged the table with his fist. 'We assumed that William Vaughn killed himself and just didn't bother to investigate Evelyn's death at all. Nisha was right. If she had been blond and blue-eyed from Bondi, then the press would have been all over it. Who cares if another poor "indigenous Australian" dies abroad? Honestly, guys, I'm feeling embarrassed and disgusted by my fellow countrymen just about now.'

There followed a silence. It was Nisha who broke it. 'In India, we have the worst crime rate against women. In China and Hong Kong, they have huge human rights issues. In America, it is still more dangerous to be black than to have cancer and the disappeared in Cambodia numbered millions in recent history. Don't worry Doug, we all aspire to be perfect, and maybe this thought and case will make us better people, if not improved detectives.'

'Yes, let's keep on the case. What have we found?' I asked, trying to bring the team back on point.

Both David and Lei had been silent during Nisha's admonition, but now David perked up. 'Well, I found that you might well have an eyewitness!'

'What!' we all said.

'Using the FBI sound analysing equipment, we found a small noise in the background. You have a good Huawei phone, Michael, remarkably good sound definition.'

'But what was the noise?' I asked.

'Once David had spotted this, I used our sound database, and it was easy from there. It was a drone,' bubbled Richie.

'No, it can't be. There are no drones allowed anywhere near the Angkor Wat region,' I said.

'Well, we then searched the internet, that's why I stole Lei from you. We tracked down a site showing illegal drone footage. It's sort of on the dark web, not searchable using normal tools and...' We hung on Richie's every word. 'Just look at this.'

He pressed a button and a massive flat-screen TV lowered from the ceiling. He played with a tablet and suddenly we were high up in the sky over the jungles of Cambodia. There was a commentary in Chinese, so we all looked to Lei.

'It says the drone is coming over the Preah Kral pagoda.' Below we could see a splendid Buddhist temple with its Dutch hat style roof, shining in gold from the dense green canopy. The drone then sped along, following a country road. 'Now we see the village of Khnang Phnum below before we turn down to the site of the Kneeling Elephant.' It was totally obscured by the trees, even as the drone dipped low over the foliage. 'Then we see the Hindu temple of Ballang.'

I asked for the image to be frozen as the drone hovered over the temple. We could clearly see a body lying on the ground, with a dark figure some metres away. As we restarted the footage, the drone whizzed on by, circling over the virgin jungle then swooping back down towards the temple. There was a dark car, but the number plate was obscured from this angle. It sped off back down the road. It seemed the drone started to cover the car leaving, but broke off the chase for another sweep of the temple, this time dropping low.

'Another tourist is sleeping off the effects of Dragon wine.' Lei continued to translate the commentary, then it stopped.

'Wow, I don't think we can identify anyone from that, but thanks guys that was tremendous work,' I said as all three beamed with pride. 'So, we can confirm the time of death, the fact it was a single murderer, and that a black vehicle was involved corroborating our witness from the Kneeling Elephant statue.'

'I'm afraid Lei and I have drawn a blank tracking William down, at least for Cambodia, as the crossing points don't have CCTV and the guards can add nothing to their earlier statements. If William hired a car, we can't see it on our systems. He seems to have slipped through the country like a ghost, as if he wasn't here at all. Nisha, Doug, have you had more luck?'

Doug waved Nisha on. 'Do you mind if I take over the screen?' A nod from Lei and Nisha connected her pad to the screen so we could see the mass of documents that they had uncovered. 'As you can see, there is quite a paper trail from Australia. First, we found the marriage certificate of the Vaughn's. This shows they only got married a few days before their trip, explaining the passports. So, we then started to look at the money, well, the wills. Interestingly, Evelyn died intestate, which, according to the local records officer, is not uncommon. As it seems she died before her husband, this should make little difference to any inheritance, as all her money would go to him.'

'I'm lost,' said Lei. 'How did she get her credit cards so quickly and what the fuck does "intestate" mean?"

Nisha put on a very expensive looking pair of glasses and read from her notes. 'It appears that getting a credit card for your partner is easy in Australia. These were shared cards; a Visa and a Mastercard. Possibly, William could have tracked her movements by following her spending?'

'That could explain how he tracked her down in Cambodia,' I said. I did so want to be able to add some local knowledge.

'And "intestate" Lei is simply dying without leaving a will. You have similar, if more restrictive, laws in China.'

We were getting information overload. I hoped Nisha could help us through this.

She continued, 'However, there is a claim by the local community that has been registered at the state office. They say that all of Evelyn's property should revert to the community. This may or may not be relevant. It is an area which appears to be both unclear and contested in law in the Northern Territories of Australia.'

I wondered where this was going. 'But was there any money to inherit?'

'Patience Michael, you will get fed soon. William was a mining engineer who had spent his entire career working for major companies, estimating deposits of rare earth elements. He had become "unemployable" according to his last company due to excessive drinking. No mean feat in Australia!'

We all laughed while Doug buried his head in his hands.

'Earlier this year he had set up his own mining company and had told many people in Naiyu that he knew where the

"Mother Lode" was, according to the lady at the Naiyu community centre I talked to. At the age of sixty-two, he suddenly married Evelyn, who was thirty-two, surprising everybody as up to this point he had held pretty strong anti-indigenous people's views.'

'So why marry her?' asked Lei.

Doug said, 'My question precisely.'

'And here we may be getting to the nub of the issue,' Nisha continued. 'Everyone we talked to said that Evelyn dreamed of travelling, that she had been fixated by the Hindu religion and, in her own way, was trying to find analogies with her indigenous culture. She was a penniless schoolteacher, although she technically owned huge stretches of desert and scrubland, which had been considered wasteland and valueless. Could this have been land William was after?'

'And?' I asked.

'And that is as far as we have got. I need to follow up on who gets the land if it does not revert to the Naiuyu community.'

'So, at that point, chaps, let's head off to supper. We have a cultural event this evening, the local force is taking us to see the night sites of Singapore. It's a three-line whip, I'm afraid,' said Bob.

We all looked confused.

'It's arcane British Parliamentary practice,' said Nisha. 'It means we must go!'

'Great, well I'd just like to thank you for your efforts today, it has been amazing, and I look forward to finding our killer tomorrow,' I said before we trooped off for the night.

I rang home and chatted with Jimmy and Jenny, my children. They were so excited that I was working with the

FBI. I don't think I have ever been held in such high esteem with my family. I didn't dare say I was the team leader, they would have ribbed me constantly as the "Big Boss" or some such nonsense. After the call, the enormity of our investigation struck me. I had been told by Commander Jones that by end of play tomorrow our team had been one of the few chosen to present back to the conference.

'A quick what happened, where we were, where are we now and what have we learnt.' He had said this as if it was a common daily occurrence. 'As the team leader, I expect you to present, though you can use your people if their expertise is required,' Bob had said to me.

I rang Cyril to give him an update; his comments were hardly reassuring.

'The top men from Phnom Penh are watching you, Michael, for Christ's sake. Don't mess up!'

I was so worried about the pressures building on me that I can't remember anything about our evening meal or entertainment and despite going to bed at ten pm having had little to drink; I didn't sleep well at all. I'm from a small town, a small country police inspector, not a high-powered international crime buster. I just wanted to get out of this and get home.

We started the next morning at seven am. I had sent a note around to everyone and had managed to get breakfast delivered to our meeting room. Neither David nor Lei looked in top shape after enjoying the free drinks on offer the previous evening. Doug and Ritchie both breezed in, followed by Nisha, who looked as if she had just walked out of a hair salon.

'How do you manage to look so good in the morning, Nisha?' I asked in a comradely spirit.

'I have a pact with the devil,' she smiled, 'and I work very hard at looking so casual. Woman lawyers must look twice as good and perform twice as well just to be treated as equals with men.'

This must also apply to the women in Cambodia, but they are not even given the chance to try.

'So, who are our suspects, then?' I asked the team now assembled as I tucked into the mountain of Asian and Western breakfast delights.

Richie stood up and took a pen over to the wall where we had all the information laid out. 'We have William Vaughn and Che Lo and A.N. Other.' He circled the last name. 'I guess the question is who A.N. Other could be?'

'Who else do we have in the files?' I asked.

Doug said, 'There is the "Nauiyu community leader", who is after Evelyn's land and, I guess, William's sister? Does she get anything?'

'Urgmuffle,' Nisha indelicately started to speak and bite into a croissant at the same time. 'Sorry,' she said, clearing her throat, then putting up her hand to stop us all from interrupting as she took a swig of coffee. 'The sister Charlotte is the sole beneficiary of William. Australian probate has just cleared and she inherits both his company and thus the land, although this is still deemed worthless.'

Lei looked better, having polished off a couple of bowls of noodles and some of the exceptional dumplings that I had tried earlier. 'But she is blonde and has a cast-iron alibi.'

'What is her alibi?' I asked. I hadn't followed up with the sister-in-law, as she seemed to have little to do with my case.

Richie said, 'According to the police reports, she was at home on her ranch when they contacted her with the news of Evelyn's death. A local policeman, Dan Phillips, found her in the fields where she was tending to her peanut crop. She had gone away after the wedding; she says she went walkabout.'

'What?' asked David.

'Oh, it's a pretty standard thing where I'm from,' said Doug. 'People get a bit wound up with life, so they just walk off into the bush. She was evidently back by the Sunday before the murder, though. And she was definitely in town on the Saturday after, as she started a fight in the only bar in town and spent an evening in the cooler.'

'What does "evidently" mean?' I asked.

'Well, no one saw her, but then her place is a bit remote. She was back on Facebook and was sending emails to the local water company about breaks in supply she had been having whilst away. But what does it matter? She couldn't have been in Cambodia killing her sister at the time.'

'And her brother's death?' asked Lei.

'Well, the police reckon he topped himself just as she was getting taken in for causing the fight. No, it can't be her,' Doug said with finality.

'And you don't fancy it was this community chief? I don't even have his name,' I asked.

'That's because he is just a lawyer based in Canberra. I expect the claim is most likely nothing more than a fishing expedition,' answered Nisha.

We all sat quietly. I thought we had had something last night, but now it seemed the ripples on the pond had stopped. Just then, Commander Jones popped his head around the door.

'Can I join?' he asked.

I took him through our findings. 'Any ideas, commander?'

'Hmm,' he said, 'once you eliminate the impossible, whatever remains, no matter how improbable, must be the truth.'

'Confucius?' asked Lei.

'Nope, Sherlock Holmes's author, Sir Arthur Conan Doyle,' Bob said. 'So, who should have done it? If they could have? And then how could they have done it? I think you have a case here where the murderer has set out to create confusion and obfuscation because the answer is so simple.'

Richie said, 'Charlotte did it, but how?'

Bob seemed happy now. 'Well, wouldn't it be useful if you had a team of people who could potentially track down a Ninja of a murderer using the most advanced of the world's electronic surveillance tools?' With that, he picked up a large gooey doughnut, which had no place on a breakfast table, took an enormous bite with unbound relish, and left us to our thoughts, closing the door delicately behind him.

Nisha was first to speak. 'OK, so Charlotte was pissed off that her brother had wed and uses this as an excuse to go walkabout, but instead bumps them both off and eventually claims her brother's company and Evelyn's land, with, we suppose, the "motherlode" hidden somewhere in it?'

'That would mean that she travelled to Cambodia, not her brother,' added Lei.

'So if we can find any sign of her during that journey, then we have her?' David checked with us all.

Could she have done this? Bob had told us that we needed to follow the great detective, and I am sure he would have loved the tools at our disposal.

'But we have no cameras at the Cambodian land borders, and getting access to either Thai or Vietnamese footage would require a massive diplomatic effort,' said David.

'What would the route she would have taken look like?' asked Richie. 'This is not exactly my neck of the woods.'

We pored over our computers for some minutes as we checked out possible routes.

'It seems the first and last legs would be via Broome or Darwin from Perth as there are so few direct flights into Northern Australia,' I said.

'I could analyse the footage for a forty-eight-hour period in no time and find her if she is there,' said Lei with great certainty.

'And the chance of Australia giving access to internal CCTV files is the same as the Poms beating us at Ozzie rules,' said Doug with even greater certainty. 'I would explain that, Richie, but we don't have the time.'

Richie looked confused.

'Yes, you are right, Doug. We need to find a more compliant government, one who would subsume the good of the one to the good of the many,' said Nisha.

'Hong Kong and China would fit that bill, but I doubt it would help us with any potential flight schedule,' said David.

'There is always Singapore,' I said.

After some checking, it seemed certain that if our murderer had had to return to Australia quickly, then the only real route would mean they would have passed through Singapore, either on the outward leg to Ho Chi Minh in Vietnam or the return from Chiang Mai in Thailand.

'I think we will need some help here. Everyone, work out the likely journey. We may need further contact points. I will try to get us access to the Singapore Changi Airport CCTV.'

Commander Jones looked at me with surprise when I tracked him down in the main hall and put in our information request. 'You need what?' he asked.

I explained our thoughts. I laid out the routes most likely taken and how they intersected with Singapore and gave him the flights we needed checking. We went together to see our hosts, who also expressed concern, especially as we were proposing to use Chinese facial recognition software in Singapore. It wasn't until after lunch that I found myself in the Minister for the Interior's office, with Commander Jones, Agent Green from the FBI, and the head of the Singapore's police authority.

'So Chief Inspector, you wish me to let a Chinese software expert interrogate our CCTV systems at Changi Airport using Chinese government software?' Put like that, I didn't feel our chances of success were good. Maybe, eventually, the Australians could do something, but from the grunts of despair from Doug, that sounded unlikely.

'And you would gain what from this? And more importantly, we would gain what from this?' He looked at me with piercingly intelligent eyes. He would make mincemeat of my Cambodian senior leaders.

'Minister,' interjected Commander Jones. 'As I understand it, we would not be on your systems, simply using your data. We would have this in an air-locked system, with no opportunity to retain any of the information, and the software would be deleted completely after use.'

'And to answer your question, minister,' I bowed. 'We would not only bring a heinous criminal to book, but prove how international cooperation can deter crime, which is the purpose of the conference that you are hosting.'

The Minister conferred quietly with his adviser. 'And it seems your group is the most likely to solve a real case?'

The FBI man cut in. 'We never expected any outcomes like this. If we could solve a case, it would be outstanding, minister.'

We were given permission! During the afternoon Lei supported David as they worked through the CCTV files until at four-thirty I got a call.

'We have her,' shouted Lei down the phone.

The rest of the afternoon was a rush of activity, pulling our solution together. Luckily, both Nisha and Richie were experts at this and took total control of the presentation. How could I have ever thought I didn't need a lawyer on an investigation? Richie's clear and incisive brain helped me put my thoughts in order; I could really use him back home, although after he told me his salary, I cooled on the idea.

David and Lei continued to work well together, perfecting the results they had obtained and ensured that they fit in with Nisha's presentation.

Doug was the most hectic, as he had to arrange everything at the Australian end. Five o'clock in Singapore was six-thirty pm in Darwin, which was a good two and a half-hour drive from Nauiyu. He gave me the thumbs up just as I was going on stage. I had persuaded Commander Jones to put us on last, so we eventually went on at six-thirty.

The three other teams who presented had all made some progress on their cases, but you could see the disappointment on the faces of the top brass who sat down on one side. It appeared that the success or failure of the conference hung on our results. In fact, they hung on my presentation. I could just imagine that the expectations for a group headed by a Cambodian were low. Only Commander Jones and the head of the police had known of our information request, and we had kept our ultimate result secret, even from them.

The team all shook hands before the start. 'Thanks, you have been spectacular,' I said to them.

I stood in front of the conference. First, I went through the case, explaining how we had used audio and advanced forensics. Although we had never found the murder weapon, Richie had dug out some footage of petite Khmer village women using their Condor knives to slice through jungle trees, demonstrating that a woman could easily have inflicted the wound. He also displayed some computer- modelled results showing the force required. His testimony all depended on the culprit being a skilled knife user. He then showed that although peanut farmers use automatic machinery for harvesting, they all have to be dextrous with the use of blades. I am sure that once we trace all her movements, we will find someone who sold her a knife.

The evidence from the phone which led to the drone footage made the entire audience groan with delight. David took them through the sound analysis, where he isolated the drone noise. He then showed how he had found the footage on the dark web. Lei then displayed the video on screen. Rarely did you get to see the murderer at the scene, and although not proof, the disguise worn by Charlotte would be great corroborating evidence.

Although we have still to prove the exact route that she took through Cambodia, I showed how by following the credit card records she could have kept up with Evelyn, waiting for the moment to strike. I also showed excerpts from Cambodia news in English, an easy to access service, which detailed all the grim details of the murderer Che Lo. I showed how Charlotte could copycat the murders, just as many of the Ripper's murders had been imitations.

I then talked about the investigation by Nisha, and how she had finally found the real value of the heavy metals discovery that William Vaughn had made. It was a vital piece of evidence that gave a clear motive for the murder. Nisha had also found that the document making the claim had been countersigned by Charlotte, confirming that she knew of the find. Nisha's explanation of inheritance law showed why Charlotte had needed it to look like her brother had died after Evelyn, otherwise, the inheritance would not go to her but to the local aboriginal community. Hopefully, the search of her home will find some DNA to substantiate this. Otherwise, it will be up to the Australian courts.

But the *pièce de résistance* was a picture, a single frame from thousands of hours of security footage which Lei's bespoke computers had sorted through. The software had analysed this in an afternoon, a task which would have taken weeks manually. There in an area no one would expect to find a camera, the ladies' restroom at Singapore Changi Airport. Our suspect. Charlotte could clearly be seen donning her disguise to impersonate her brother.

'So, ladies and gentlemen, at this very moment, colleagues of our team member Doug Houet are arresting Charlotte for the murder of her sister-in-law Evelyn in

Cambodia. We expect that they will then soon be able to link her with her brother's murder and allow us to close the file on not one, but two cases.' The applause was thunderous. We were treated as heroes by all attending.

Commander Jones came to me afterwards and said enigmatically, 'I knew you could crack this one, Michael. Well done!'

Back in our office in Siem Reap, I finished giving my report to Cyril and Doctor Pang. My wife and daughter loved the perfumes I had brought, and the good doctor had paid me for the Chanel no.5 for his wife. As for Jimmy, he was over the moon with his Lego farming set, although confused at the sight of a black and white cow. I passed over my expenses and said, 'Nothing from the minibar, Cyril.'

'You know that if it wasn't for the praise we have had internationally on this one you would be in real trouble with the security services,' Cyril said sagely. 'But I think keeping a low profile will be difficult now. I have heard that you are being talked of in high places, possibly a new assignment is the wind.'

'So where is this fine whisky from? Eighteen-year-old Glenfiddich is not cheap Michael,' interrupted Doctor Pang.

'A gift. It came with a note which said "To my Asian Sherlock Holmes, may we work together again. Commander Jones".'

'Well pass it over, it's no good staying in the bottle!' said Cyril.

'Yes sir,' I agreed.

Fin

The Confession

My name is Michael Suon, Chief Inspector of the Cambodian National Police and I have committed murder. I have travelled over two hours from Siem Reap to the small town of Prah Sat where I confess to a priest who I have never met before.

The church is an old French colonial building and is based within a compound surrounded by a high stone wall. It may well have been a convent in the past, but there are precious few nuns in Cambodia now.

The confessional is made of some old exotic dark wood, no doubt now on some modern conservation list. There is no one else in the church. The confessional booth is available as a small light signifies that a priest is waiting. I pull back the black curtain, sit on the bare wooden bench and press my face close to the meshed screen. I can hear his heavy breathing.

'Bless me, Father, for I have sinned. It has been two weeks since my last confession,' I say. The priest waits for me to continue. 'I can trust you not to share this confession, can't I, Father?' It would seem an absurd question normally, but the tale I am going to tell could ruin me.

'The sacrament is sacred. Have no fear. You are confessing to God here, not to man,' he replies reassuringly.

'I have committed murder.'

There is silence from the other side of the screen, then, 'You had better tell me your story, my son. I need to understand the context of your sin. Don't worry about time; I am free all day.'

I take a deep breath and start to recount the previous forty-eight hours.

'Well, my wife and I have been having problems. She is a simple village girl and doesn't always understand the strains that I have at work. I can't simply come home at five pm and close the door. I am a police chief inspector and that means I am on call twenty-four hours a day.' I wait for the priest to acknowledge me.

'Just keep going, my son. This isn't a conversation. I am listening,' he says finally.

'Well, we had just finished a major case. I had been working with Nong Kimny, the head of the narcotics squad, a very efficient and outrageously talented man who is a high flier in the national police. I had been seconded to give in-depth local knowledge of the area to the north of Siem Reap, where the drugs were thought to be coming from.

In the end, we caught a big fish, head of a significant criminal gang, and Nong took him back to Phnom Penh in a blaze of glory. My team was highly praised, I was given a big tick by my boss and gifted an unused high-end Huawei y9 phone which had been found whilst searching a hideout. It was not needed for evidence and would normally have been thrown away. Being given, it was not exactly legal but common practice and approved by Cyril, the regional police chief.

Flicking through the phone to check that there were no contacts on it, I came across an app called "Fantasy Wife". I dimly recalled my colleagues talking about this, how they wished they could afford it, so I clicked on through. It was a barely disguised escort agency, with semi-pornographic pictures of women undertaking household chores. I guess my first confession must be that I was aroused by it.

I should have taken the phone back to IT to clear it. Instead, I was intrigued, so I followed through the link thinking that it could never be traced back to me as I would be putting a new SIM into the phone and replacing the pay-as-you-go one, which was in place.

By clicking through, I was taken to the apps calendar page, which flashed up a current pre-paid appointment for that evening at seven pm. Looking at my watch, I had time to have a quick bite to eat before walking to the address which was across town, behind the Park Hyatt Hotel, a very posh area.

I don't know what I had in mind as I rang the bell. All I had been thinking was to look out for CCTV in case we could catch whoever had originally booked this girl. I think I meant this to be a work trip, or am I just kidding myself? As soon as the door opened, I was thunderstruck, my mouth fell open, and I fell in love. Her beauty was not that of a supermodel or glamour girl, although she certainly could have been one. It was just that she was perfect. I was so stunned I didn't know what to say and lost my opportunity to show my card with police identification.

"I'm…" I started to say my name.

"Hush, we don't have names here," she said flashing me a pearlescent smile. Her mouth was highlighted with dark luscious lipstick, and her perfect white teeth were exposed as her lips parted. "Just call me darling," she said and blushed, establishing that she wore little makeup as her skin was naturally flawless.

I had considered what to do if she had been a youngster. It would have made the whole process so easy, but at a guess, I would have said she was at least twenty-two. Surely old enough to make her own decisions in life? She motioned me in, pecked me on the cheek, and slipped off my jacket. I was overwhelmed by her rich perfume, which seemed to exude woody spice and summer roses.

"Sit down and relax," she said.

I did as I was told and found her unlacing my shoes and massaging my feet. I began to speak again, but she interrupted me and said, "Calm, first things first. Can we tap apps?" I got out the phone, and she showed me how to complete our transaction by touching it to hers.

"What do you want to drink? No, let me guess, whisky?" She poured a good couple of inches of Scotch, Glenlivet I think, and gave it to me in a crystal tumbler.'

The priest intervened at this point, 'What was your intention at this moment, my son?'

'I honestly don't know, Father. All I knew then was this was what I was due from an ideal spouse. I shouldn't come home from working all day to be assaulted by screaming arguing kids and to be harangued by a wife who had a shopping list of faults for me to attend to and urgent jobs to be undertaken, whilst being bombarded with a torrent of abuse due to the lateness of my arrival.

'Here, I was being treated as a husband should be. I was being pampered and soothed, massaged and given a relaxing drink. I didn't think I needed more. I hadn't even thought of sex. Well, of course I had, vaguely. My wife and I hadn't had sex for a month, and before that, whenever I touched her, she winced or complained. She went rigid at the first sign of a sexual advance and simply suffered my caresses. I got nothing more than I would from a cheap sex doll from the market and certainly gained better relief from masturbation than from coupling. So, the thought of sex with a compliant woman was high on my mind. I had never envisaged it would be with someone who looked so good.

'I was conflicted, though. I had never cheated on my wife, never slept with anyone other than her. I also realised that this girl was a professional sex worker, so could be riddled with disease beneath her beautiful shell. She could also have been a sex slave, being kept in this apartment like a princess in a gilded cage. Could I have sex with someone who I didn't love and who didn't care for me? As far as your question, Father, I believe that my intention was not to have intercourse but…

'There was a tap at the door. She giggled and said, "Oh good, presents." Clapping her hands together like an excited teenager, her professional, mature wife image slipped a touch.

'I thought that her payment given to her at the door was probably drugs. I couldn't see any obvious signs on her, but then prostitutes often ensured that their clients couldn't see their vices. I got to get up, but she stopped me saying, "No, no, no, I still want a five-star rating and I know how to get one…"

'She took out a condom from a drawer and said, "It's always best", then knelt in front of me, slipped my trousers down and…'

'I can do without the details, my son. I assume she performed fellatio. We do know what it is,' interjected the priest.

'Yes, well after I had arrived, she took the condom, tied a knot around it, gave me a gentle wipe then said, "I'll just take care of this" and I assumed she went to dispose of it.

'I sat there in the chair with my trousers down, I took a long draft of the whisky closed my eyes and relived the recent experience. Unbelievably, I slipped off to sleep. I was woken after a few minutes as the whisky glass had slipped from my hand and was now dripping fine malt on to my exposed thigh. I shot up, pulling on my trousers, slightly disorientated from the booze.

'She hadn't come back from the bathroom, so I went looking. The apartment was a wonderful place with two bedrooms and great views of the Royal Palace down by the river. The master bed was covered in gold satin sheets edged with some suede material; it all looked vastly expensive. What I assumed to be the bathroom door was locked, but was simple to open as the bolt mechanism had a slot on the outside which, given a screwdriver, could be turned. At the time, I thought that this would be useful at home as it would stop my teenage daughter from locking herself in the bathroom.

'I was horrified when I opened the door as the young lady was slumped in the corner. Scattered all around was her drug paraphernalia. She had no pulse and was cooling quickly. Up close, I could now see that there were signs of previous injections. They had, however, been covered up by some excellent cosmetics. Having been to a hundred crime scenes, it was second nature for me not to touch anything or leave my own traces. As there was nothing I could do for this young girl, I selfishly just thought of myself.

'I checked the bin, but she must have flushed the condom down the toilet, however, I picked out the discarded wrapper. I then backtracked through the flat, wiping anything I could have touched. I washed the glass, ensured I hadn't left obvious hairs on the chair and when I was sure I had checked everywhere, I walked slowly through the apartment, inspecting again. When I left, it looked like the girl had been on her own. As an investigator, if I had seen this scene, my first question would be why she had taken drugs in the bathroom and not in a more comfortable place. As it was, I didn't understand why she had to shoot up with me there? She hadn't had any signs of a desperate need; I had never seen such an in-control junkie.

'I left, once more ensuring I was not captured on CCTV, walked back across the bridge and home, thankful that I hadn't used a car. On the way, I bought a new sim from a local vendor. I had decided to keep the phone, but as backup only. I erased the "Fantasy Wife" app, then reset the phone to factory settings. I had planned possibly to give the phone to my daughter but shuddered at the thought now. On arriving, I called out to everyone that I was tired, hungry, and in a foul mood. I retreated to the garage, which I had been turning into my man cave, leaving the car to rest dangerously in the road at night.

'Jenny, my daughter, came down with a bowl of pork and rice and an Angkor beer. "Mummy is not feeling very well," she told me.

'I thanked her for the food, told her to send my love to mummy, and said I would be up after they were all in bed. I knew that both Bophra, my wife and I were using our children as pawns in some matrimonial battle. I felt distraught that I was damaging them, but I couldn't just give in and kow-tow to my wife's parochial ways.

'My son Jimmy then came down. He has Down's and although that means he is technically stupid, when it comes to people, he can be very astute. After playing cars for half an hour at my feet, saying nothing, he said: "Mummy does love you, daddy." He then gave me a hug and went back to the flat. Even he was being affected by our behaviour. Who am I kidding? My behaviour.'

I fall silent, contemplating my actions.

'I'm sorry,' said the priest, interrupting my thoughts. 'I can't see how you murdered that girl.'

'You are right, Father. It is not her I murdered, although I'm sure I've racked up a healthy total of penances already.'

I could hear the priest chuckle.

'I was in the office early the next morning. I was pretty sure that I couldn't be linked with the girl's death, but as so much hung on this, my reputation, my job and my marriage, I wanted to make certain. It wasn't until mid-morning that the call came through of a body in a classy flat in what looked like a drug overdose. Pretending to be reluctant, I told my boss Cyril that I should check, just in case it was linked to the case I had recently finished.

"You are a martyr to the cause," he replied and went on stamping his name on a pile of departmental expense chits.

'I arrived at the flat, which was full of CSI officers. These were generally the brightest and the best of the men on the force. They all spent a couple of years in this special unit in lieu of any proper training. It was also generally thought that new officers were less likely to steal things from crime scenes than older, more seasoned men. From the number here, I guessed that more than a couple of the white-suited individuals were on the lookout for easy pickings rather than clues, which, for me at the time, was fine.

'After I arrived, the number of officers soon diminished. I have a reputation as a hard arse, by-the-book man. If only they knew how I felt when I walked into that flat that morning.

Our head of forensics, Doctor Sonith Pang, was in the bathroom, hunched over the girl's body. Although she had been dead some twelve hours, she still looked beautiful. The luscious red lipstick glistened against her cold pale skin.

"Well, Doctor, what do we know?" I asked.

"She's been dead a good twelve hours, at least."

"Any likely cause?"

"If I were the type of person to make assumptions, then the fact that she has a tourniquet loosely wrapped around her arm, a syringe in her hand and a pile of chemicals that look suspiciously illegal spread around her, I might be persuaded to conjecture a drug connection. But you knew that before you came, so why are you here? Drugs are not your thing."

'A wave of panic went through me. Was I that obvious? Calming myself, I said, "Just checking the linkage to the big op we have been on. Thoroughness is my watchword, doctor."

"Well, I don't think there will be anything left around to steal from the flat, Chief Inspector," he replied caustically. "I will know if anything is other than it seems by tomorrow. Until then, we will look after this poor young thing."

"Any signs of sexual intercourse?" I asked to ensure I followed my standard questioning.

"I couldn't see any, but there was an empty condom wrapper in the bin." I felt a shiver down my spine. I was sure I had checked there, damn it, was I so careless?

'The spry old doctor stood up. "Well, I will have more by tomorrow. She has left enough heroin sprinkled around here for me to have oodles to sample."

'As I left the girl's apartment, a message popped up on my old phone. I was loath to use my new one. "Revisiting the scene?" The message said. I stumbled as I realised that Someone was watching me. "You left your calling card," a second message quickly followed.

'I thought about answering. Instead, I walked back to my scooter. Traffic mid-morning was too much for any sane person to use a car in town.

'As I sat down and pressed the ignition a third message came through, "Meet me 8pm Phnom Bakheng or else".

'It was hardly the most elegant threat, but it was clear enough. Somehow, someone had been watching me the previous night. They must have found the used condom with my semen protected in its knotted sheath in the toilet system and then planted a new wrapper in the bin. I knew I had taken it out of the bin. And now they intended to blackmail me.

'I spent the day in a stew, thinking through and discarding a hundred plans. At least it gave me time to organise myself a well-planned alibi, by complaining bitterly to anyone who would listen that I had to meet my uncle in Damdek, a small village an hour to the east of town.'

'How was that an alibi?' the priest asked.

'Well, my uncle is a secret dementia case. He would swear blind I had been there if asked. It has saved me from my wife before. I think it was a hundred Hail Mary's the last time I confessed to it.'

There is no response then...

'You were planning to kill your blackmailer? Preparing an alibi to avoid being caught? Not casual murder but premeditated?' he says, sounding shocked.

'You are right, Father. I could have had murder in mind. I hadn't thought of it as premeditated. I suppose it makes my ultimate penance even worse?'

I resume my monologue.

'At six, I rang home to say I would be late again, and then, using a stolen moped from the pile of confiscated bikes in the police yard, I slipped off to the Phnom Bakheng temple. As a seasoned officer, I knew a hundred ways to hot-wire a moped, and the ones in the yard were normally confiscated bikes which had been jump-started a hundred times before. I didn't want my car being seen anywhere in the temple complex, and anyway, mopeds can go places cars can't.

'Having been brought up in Siem Reap, I know every route through the Angkor temple complex. Avoiding the guards was easy and as sunset had passed the majority of tourists had left with only the last few stragglers being escorted out. Phnom Bakheng, as its name suggests, is a hilltop shrine, a large platform with great views of Angkor Wat at sunset. I wanted to be there before my adversary turned up, but alas he was already ensconced in one of the temple turrets.

"Who are you?" I shouted, "I'm here to do a deal."

A man emerged in the dim light. I was shocked to see that I knew my nemesis, Sergeant Munny Chanda.'

'Who?' asked the priest.

'Munny Chanda, he used to work for me before moving on to military operations with General Cho. Do you know him?'

'No, no,' said the priest, 'I thought you said someone else.'

'From across the ancient platform, he said, "So, Chief Inspector, I appear to have you by the balls, or at least their contents." He was swinging the knotted condom at me. "I have a few jobs that you can help me with to compensate for the loss of one of my best girls."

"I thought you were an errand boy for the general now. What are you doing with prostitutes?" I shouted. The temple was deserted save for the two of us. The temple guards generally just kept to the perimeter of the main Angkor complex at night. No one in their right mind would be up here once all the tourists had been cleared away.

"Don't worry, I keep the general happy, and like a good leader, he doesn't mind his men making a bit on the side."

'It was getting very dark now with only moonlight occasionally illuminating the scene as clouds blew past, I didn't think he had his gun out, so, I pulled mine and said, "OK, drop that and put your hands up, I'm wearing a wire and am arresting you."

"You wouldn't dare," he said, and went for his gun.'

'And you shot and killed him?' said the priest. 'Look, we must wrap this up, I do need to get on.'

I looked at my phone, which was on silent, and smiled. 'Yes, I agree Father we do need to wrap this up. And no, I didn't kill him. He is alive and well and singing like a canary in our cells back in Siem Reap.'

'But you said you were confessing to murder?'

'Yes, I fear I have to add lying in a confessional to my list.'

'But...'

'You see, he told us that the man who supplied him with prostitutes was a nasty piece of work. That the girls were taken from small villages, often sold by their parents. This man then abused them, pumped them full of drugs and conditioned them into believing that they wanted to work for him. The good sergeant informed me that there was a new batch of girls ready to be transferred to Phnom Penh, and that they were hidden in a place beyond the reach of a search warrant. We were warned that if we tried to storm the site, the girls would be killed. So we needed to distract him somehow.'

Corporal Cheng pulls back the curtain from the priest's side of the confessional and says, 'Father Joseph, I am arresting you for people trafficking.'

'But I'm a priest. I was only helping those girls.'

'Have you found any others, Corporal?' I ask.

'Yes sir, twelve girls in all.'

'Well, make sure they are well cared for and take him back to the station. I've had enough talking to him for now. I will deal with him in the morning.'

Back at the station, I sit with Doctor Pang and my boss, Cyril. We are in his office annexe, which has a large cabinet where he keeps his drink. We are sitting in his antique leather chairs around a small circular table, which was said to have been liberated from a British industrialist's house by the Khmer Rouge.

'What did you say to this chap, the fake priest?' Cyril asks. 'Cheng told me you kept him tied up for over an hour whilst they searched the church and grounds for the girls.'

'I just told him what he wanted to hear, boss. I had a chance to live out the fantasies of a cop turned bad, and I rather sickened myself in the process. I do believe I will have to recite a lot of Hail Mary's in penance when I next take a real confession. Mostly for impure thoughts. I was grateful when Cheng sent me a text. I was running out of story and don't know what I would have said next.'

'Well, I say pass me that bottle of Laphroaig that I liberated from that poor girl's flat yesterday. I could do with another large drink,' says Pang.

'Isn't that theft, doctor?' I ask.

'Good Lord, no. It is criminal reparations!' he replies aghast.

'And as for the dead girl?' asks Cyril.

'I'm afraid we have another batch of tainted heroin, expect more untimely deaths,' the doctor replies, swirling an injudicious amount of whisky around his tumbler.

'To another couple of bad guys off the streets. Well done, Michael.' Cyril toasts, and we all take a long swallow.

Fin